I0533979

Love at Paddington by William Pett Ridge

William Pett Ridge was born at Chartham, near Canterbury, Kent on 22nd April 1859.

His family's resources were certainly limited. His father was a railway porter, and his son, after schooling in Marden, Kent became a clerk in a railway clearing house. The hours were long and arduous, but self improvement was his goal. After working from nine until seven o'clock he attended evening classes at Birkbeck Literary and Scientific Institute and then he would write.

From 1891 his humourous sketches were published in the St James's Gazette, the Idler, Windsor Magazine and other literary periodicals of the day. He was heavily influenced by Dickens and critics thought he might be his successor.

Pett Ridge published his first novel in 1895, A Clever Wife. By his fifth novel, Mord Em'ly, three years later, his success was obvious. His writing was written from the perspective of those born with no privilege and relied on talent to find humour and sympathy in his portrayal of working class life.

Today Pett Ridge and other East End novelists including Arthur Nevinson, Arthur Morrison & Edwin Pugh are grouped together as the Cockney Novelists.

With his success Pett Ridge gave generously of both time and money to charity. In 1907 he founded the Babies Home at Hoxton, one of several children's organisations

His circle considered Pett Ridge to be one of life's natural bachelors. In 1909 they were rather surprised therefore when he married Olga Hentschel.

As the 1920's arrived Pett Ridge added to his popularity with the movies. Four of his books were adapted into films.

Pett Ridge now found the peak of his fame had passed. He still managed to produce a book a year but was falling out of fashion and favour with the reading public. His canon runs to over sixty novels and short story collections as well as many pieces for magazines and periodicals.

William Pett Ridge died, on 29th September 1930, at his home, Ampthill, Willow Grove, Chislehurst, at the age of 71.

Index of Contents

LOVE AT PADDINGTON

CHAPTER I

Children had been sent off to Sunday school, and the more conscientious reached that destination; going in, after delivering awful threats and warnings to those who preferred freedom of thought and a stroll down Edgware Road in the direction of the Park. As a consequence, in the streets off the main thoroughfare leading to Paddington Station peace and silence existed, broken only by folk who, after the principal meal of the week, talked in their sleep. Praed Street was different. Praed Street plumed itself on the fact that it was always lively, ever on the move, occasionally acquainted with royalty. Even on a Sunday afternoon, and certainly at all hours of a week-day, one could look from windows at good racing, generally done by folk impeded by hand luggage who, as they ran, glanced suspiciously at every clock, and gasped, in a despairing way, "We shall never do it!" or, optimistically, "We shall only just do it!" or, with resignation, "Well, if we lose this one we shall have to wait for the next."

Few establishments were open in Praed Street, shutters were up at the numerous second-hand shops, and at the hour of three o'clock p.m. the thirst for journals at E. G. Mills's (Established 1875) was satisfied; the appetite for cigars, cigarettes, and tobacco had scarcely begun. Now and again a couple of boys, who had been reading stories of wild adventure in the Rocky Mountains, dashed across the road, upset one of Mrs. Mills's placard boards, and flew in opposite directions, feeling that although they might not have equalled the daring exploits of their heroes in fiction, they had gone as far as was possible in a country hampered by civilization.

"Young rascals!" said Mrs. Mills, coming back after repairing one of these outrages. The shop had a soft, pleasing scent of tobacco from the brown jars, marked in gilded letters "Bird's Eye" and "Shag" and "Cavendish," together with the acrid perfume of printer's ink. "Still, I suppose we were all young once. Gertie," raising her voice, "isn't it about time you popped upstairs to make yourself good-looking? There's no cake in the house, and that always means some one looks in unexpectedly to tea."

No answer.

"Gertie! Don't you hear me when I'm speaking to you?"

"Beg pardon, aunt. I was thinking of something else."

"You think too much of something else, my dear," said Mrs. Mills persuasively. "I was saying to a customer, only yesterday, that you don't seem able lately to throw off your work when you've finished. You keep on threshing it out in your mind. And it's all very well, to a certain extent, but there's a medium in all things." Mrs. Mills went to the half-open door, that was curtained only in regard to the lower portion. "Trimming a hat," she cried protestingly. "Oh, my dear, and to think your mother was a Wesleyan Methodist. Before she came to London, I mean."

Her niece surveyed the work at arm's length. "I've done all I want to do to it," she said.

Mrs. Mills ordered the hat to be put on that she might ascertain whether it suited, and this done, and guarded approval given, asked to be allowed to try it on her own head. Here, again, the results, inspected in the large mirror set in a narrow wooden frame above the mantelpiece, gained commendation; Mrs. Mills declared she would feel inclined to purchase a similar hat, only that Praed Street might say she was looking for a second husband. Besides, she never went out.

"Your poor mother was just as handy with her needle as what you are. We'd go along together to have a look at the shops in Oxford Street, and the moment she returned home, she'd set to work, and alter something to make it look fashionable." Mrs. Mills sighed. "Little good it brought her, though, in the long run."

"I am sure," remarked the girl quickly, "it never brought her any harm."

"Didn't help to get hold of anybody better than your father, at any rate. But they're both gone, and it's no use talking."

Some one entered the shop.

"Your friend Miss Radford," she announced. "Now there won't be a chance for any one else to speak."

The visitor justified the prophecy, by entering the parlour with a breathless "Oh, I've got such news!" checking herself on encountering Mrs. Mills. Mrs. Mills asked, with reserve, concerning the health of Miss Radford's mother, and mentioned (not apparently for the first time) that the lady, in her opinion, ought to be living on a gravel soil. Miss Radford, obviously suffering from repressed information, promised to deliver the advice, word for word, and in the meantime gave her own warm thanks.

"Old nuisance!" she remarked, as the half-curtained door closed. "I wonder how you can put up with her."

"My aunt is very good to me."

"Isn't it a pity," said the visitor inconsequently, "that you're so short? Well, not exactly short, but certainly only about middle height. I think"—she glanced at the mirror complacently—"my idea is it's partly because I'm tall that I attract so much notice. I'm sure the way they gaze round after I'm gone by—Well, it used to make me feel quite confused, but I've got over that. You don't have to put up with such experiences, Gertie."

"Afraid I forget to turn to see if they're looking."

"You've got rather a thoughtless disposition," agreed the other. "Once or twice lately, when I've been telling you things that I don't tell to everybody, it's struck me that you've been scarcely listening." The door was closed, but Miss Radford verified this before proceeding. "What do you think?" she asked in an awed voice. "Whatever do you think? Two of my old ones have met. Met at a smoking concert apparently. And they somehow started talking, and my name cropped up, and," tearfully, "they've written me such a unkind letter, with both their names to it. On the top of it all, the latest one caught sight of me yesterday afternoon, dressing the window at our establishment, so that he won't put in an appearance at the Marble Arch this evening."

"Why not?"

"Because I told him I was an artist. Said I had a picture in the Royal Academy the year before last."

"You are rather foolish at times, aren't you?"

"I wish, darling," wailed Miss Radford, "that you could tell me something I don't know."

The clock on the mantelpiece struck the half-hour, and Mrs. Mills's niece, suddenly alarmed, said she would not be absent for more than ten minutes, an announcement the visitor received with an incredulous shake of the head. As a fact, Gertie returned in five minutes fully apparelled, to discover Miss Radford improved in spirits and ready for more conversation.

"A new blouse?" she cried, interrupting herself. "And you never told me. Gertie Higham," solemnly, "this isn't what I call friendship."

The girl went straight through the shop, and looking up and down Praed Street, remarked to Mrs. Mills that it intended to be a fine evening. The elder lady said it was high time Gertie found a young man to take her out; the girl answered composedly that perhaps Mr. Trew might call and do her this service.

"Or Fred Bulpert?" remarked the aunt pointedly.

"No," she answered, "not Mr. Bulpert, thank you. Mr. Trew is different."

"He isn't the man he was when I first knew him."

"I like him because he's the man he is."

She turned quickly at the sound of a deep, husky voice. Mr. Trew, on the mat, opened his arms at sight of her, and beamed with a face that was like the midday sun; she took his sleeve and pulled him to the pavement.

"At five minutes to five," she whispered urgently, "you're going to take me for a walk in Hyde Park."

"At four fifty-five to the minute," he agreed. "What's the game, may I kindly ask?"

"I'll tell you later on."

"I hadn't noticed it," he said loudly, re-entering the shop, "until my attention was drawed to it by the little missy here. But there it is right enough on the playcards. 'Motor omnibuses for London.'" He shook his head, and, leaning across the counter, addressed Mrs. Mills. "Light of my life, sunshine of my existence—"

"Don't you begin your nonsense," ordered the lady, not displeased.

"—And sweetheart when a boy, I warn you against putting any of your ill-gotten gains into that sort of speculation. They may perhaps start one from the Elephant and it'll get about as fur as the Obelisk, and there it'll stick. And they'll have to take it to pieces, and sell it for scrap iron. I know what I'm talking about."

"That's unusual in your case," said Mrs. Mills.

"I get light-headed when I see you," explained Mr. Trew. "I was took like it the first time I ran across you up in the gallery of the old Princess's, seeing 'Guinea Gold,' and you've had the same effect on me ever since. What's more, you glory in it. You're proud of the wonderful influence you exercise over me. And all I get out of you is a 'aughty smile."

"The fact is," declared Mrs. Mills, "you get too much attention from the ladies. It spoils you!"

"See how she spurns me," he cried, turning to Gertie. "You wouldn't treat a gentleman like that, would you, missy? You wouldn't play football with an honest, loving heart, I'm sure. Oh, come on," with pretended desperation, "let's have a cigar, and try to forget all about it. A twopenny one; same as you sell to members of the House of Lords."

"You're staying to tea," suggested Mrs. Mills, allowing him to make a selection from a box.

"I've got to leave just before five o'clock. Going to take the little missy here out for a promenade."

"Now that is kind and thoughtful of you," declared the other. "With all your silliness, you're not half a bad sort. Gertie, go in and lay the table."

Miss Radford, after inspecting the new-comer over the half-curtain, decided to leave, although, as she pointed out, this was an opportunity for enjoying her company that rarely occurred. In confidence, the young woman remarked that what she hoped might happen at a future date was that she would meet some one possessing a disengaged brother, in which case she guaranteed to bring all her influence to bear in favour of Gertie Higham. Gertie said this was kind, and Miss Radford mentioned that she always felt ready to do a favour whenever she happened to be in good spirits.

The three sat at table, with Mrs. Mills in a position that commanded a view of the shop. Mr. Trew had brought a bag of prawns in the tail-pocket of his coat, secured, he asserted, after enormous trouble and expense from the sea coast of Marylebone Road that very afternoon; they were, anyway, good prawns, and went admirably with thin bread and butter, and Gertie would have eaten more but for anxiety concerning progress of the hands of the clock. Mr. Trew, discussing the products of the sea, regretted that he was bound, by his work, to London—

"Horses is my occupation," he said, "but the ocean's my hobby."

—And derided town, charging it with stuffiness in this month of August, and moreover empty. He wished he were on the pier at Southend, or at Margate, or at any place, in fact, where he might see the waves rolling in and rolling out again, and shy pebbles at them.

"Gertie could have had her holiday this month," remarked Mrs. Mills, glancing with pride at her niece, "but she preferred not. I don't feel sure whether she did right or whether she did wrong in giving them up. There's more unlikely places than a seaside boarding-house to pick up a future husband." She gave details of a case of a young woman living in Harrow Road, who, in the summer of 1900, met at Eastbourne a gentleman with one arm, invalided home from the war; an engagement immediately followed. Later, the girl discovered he was already married, and that he had gone away from his wife and children, taking with him the compensation given to him by his employers, a firm of builders at Willesden.

"I expect the missy is keeping her eyes open, if the truth was known."

"But no definite results," contended Mrs. Mills. "That's what I complain of. At her age I had three after me."

"This was long before I came on the scene," explained Mr. Trew to Gertie; "otherwise there would have been bloodshed. Is this meal ad lib., or do I have to pay extra for another cup of tea?"

"I don't want her to worry about it; I only want her to keep it in view. What I should like more than anything would be to see a young man who was fond of her come in here, at a time like this, and take his piece of bread and butter, fold it, enjoy it, and sing to us afterwards."

"You're certain about that, aunt?"

"Providing he had a decent voice." The shop bell rang. Mrs. Mills half rose and recognized the customer. "We are now about to get all the news of the neighbourhood," she said desolately.

Gertie anticipated her, and, going in, served the lady with a copy of Fireside Love Stories. Returned with an imperative message.

"I shall have to see her," admitted Mrs. Mills. "She won't be happy until she gets some piece of scandal off her mind."

"Fair one," said Trew, with a wave of his hand, "every moment will seem like a century until you return!"

Gertie was fixing her newly-trimmed hat with the aid of the mirror, and Mr. Trew was describing an accident witnessed the day before near Hyde Park corner, when sound of commotion came from the street; he seized his peaked cap and hurried through the shop. Gertie followed. Conversation between the two ladies had been interrupted by the same cause and they were outside the doorway, looking on at a small crowd that acted as escort to an ambulance in charge of two policemen; the aim of every one appeared to be to snatch the privilege of securing a view of the man partly hidden by the brown hood of the conveyance. Mrs. Mills sent the customer across to obtain particulars, and remarking cheerfully to Mr. Trew and the girl, "You two off? Don't be late back, mind!" turned to the more interesting subject. Children were running up from side streets, grateful for anything likely to break the serenity of the afternoon.

"If he's damaged hisself," said Mr. Trew, as the ambulance stopped at the hospital, "he's going to the right place to get repaired."

"It's to be hoped he has friends."

"Everybody's got the friends they deserve to have. Are we going the direction to suit you, missy, or would you rather have gone Edgware Road way?"

"Let's turn down London Street," she suggested. "It will be quiet there. I've something to tell you." She rolled her parasol carefully. "And I want your help, Mr. Trew."

Three youths near the underground station, with apparently no urgent occupation, came forward hopefully on seeing Gertie; detecting the fact that she was in the company of a big, burly man, they had to pretend a sudden interest in a shuttered window. The two, going into Norfolk Square, walked on the narrow pavement near the railings of the garden.

"Mr. Trew, I've got a young man!"

"That's the best news," he exclaimed heartily, "I've heard this summer!"

"And I want somehow to get him asked indoors. Once aunt sees him and hears him talk, it will be all right. But I'm nervous about it, and I don't know how to manage."

"This," he said, holding up a forefinger, "is just where old Harry Trew comes in. This is exactly the sort of job he's fitted for. If he hadn't took up with another occupation he'd have found himself by this time in the Foreign Office. Do you want it arranged for to-night?"

"Please!"

"Right you are! You're going to meet him, I take it, presently. You asked me to come out with you simply as an excuse for that purpose. Very well, then. I've got a standing invite, as you very well know, to drop in at the nine o'clock meal any Sunday evening I like. Your aunt expects me." The forefinger became emphatic. "You simply arrange for him to meet me, say, outside the Met. at ten minutes to the hower; I shall be carrying a Lloyd's in my right hand. I brings him along," continued Mr. Trew exultantly; "I introduces him as a young personal friend of mine that I met on the steamer going to Clacton, year before last. Your aunt says at once that any friend of mine is a friend of her'n. You and him pretend not to know each other, but you gradually become acquainted, and your aunt asks him, at the finish, to look in again. Does that sound all right, or can you suggest a better plan?"

"It's splendid," she cried.

"I think," he continued, "I shall mention in the course of the evening that his father was the best friend I ever had in the world. When I was in a slight financial difficulty once, his father—your young man's father, I mean—came to my assistance. And him not well off neither. Turning-point of my life. But for that help I should, likely enough, have gone down, and down, and down." He looked at her for approval. "What's wrong with that?"

"He's a gentleman!"

Mr. Trew gazed for a few moments at a baby in a perambulator.

"I was born in 'fifty-five, the year of the Crimea War," he said deliberately, "and if my mother had had her way, I sh'd have been christened Sebastopol, which wouldn't have been any catch to a public man like myself. If I'm spared till next year, I shall be celebrating my jubilee, and all London will be illuminated, I expect, with military troops lining the streets. But what I want to tell you, missy, is that, all that time, I've never seen any good resulting from a girl in your position of life becoming friendly with any chap who was considerably above her in regard to what we call social status. On the other hand, I've seen harm come from it."

"There's going to be none in my case," she said quickly.

"I know, I know! I'm perfectly sure of that. That is to say, I'm absolutely certain that is your view now. I can't quite explain what I mean to any one of your age and your sex. If I was a well-educated man"—here he took off his cap and rubbed the top of his head with the peak—"I could find words to wrop it up somehow. The long and the short of it is, you relinquish the idea. To oblige me"—persuasively—"and to gratify your aunt, who's been pretty good to you since you were a child—"

"I don't forget that."

"—And for your own peace of mind in the future, give it all up, and you wait a bit until you find some one belonging to your own set."

"There isn't the distance between the sets there used to be," she argued.

He took hold of the railings with both hands, and tried to shake them in an effort of thought.

"What's the young chap's name?"

"I don't know."

"There you are!"—with gloomy triumph—"don't that prove the truth of everything I've been saying?"

"He doesn't know mine."

"That isn't an argument."

"Quite so," the girl agreed. "It's only a statement of fact. He will tell me his name directly I ask him, and I shall tell him my name the moment he asks me."

"No occupation, I suppose?"

"He works for his living."

"Then," turning reproachfully upon her, "what did you mean by saying he was a gentleman, and upsetting me to this extent?"

"He is a gentleman," persisted Gertie. "I can tell the difference."

Mr. Trew sighed, and took out his watch. Gertie glanced at it.

"I must go," she said. "I promised to meet him not far from the shop at half-past."

"I'd do anything to help you, missy," he declared, "because I like you. And it's just because I like you that I don't feel particular inclined to assist him. He ought to keep to his own sphere. There's a lot of talk about breaking down the barriers that divide one class from another, but, I tell you, it's a job that wants very careful handling. And I've got as much sense as most, and I rather enjoy interfering with other people's affairs, but this is an undertaking I don't care to tackle. You'll excuse me for speaking my mind, won't you? It's a habit I've got into."

"It's a good habit," said Gertie. "I practise it myself."

On the return, Mr. Trew, cap now at the back of his head, and his rubicund face bearing indications of seriousness, pointed out that the girl was in a berth in Great Titchfield Street, which he described as not so dusty, earning twenty-five shillings a week, and with Saturday afternoons and Sundays free; a good home, and everything ready for her when she returned, tired out, at night; first-class feeding, able to dress well. Mr. Trew, without daring to say whether he was right or whether he was wrong, begged to suggest there were many girls worse treated by fortune; it did seem to him that these advantages ought not to be given up lightly.

"There he is!" she cried excitedly. "Across there. Near the second-hand furniture shop."

"Your aunt's calling you," he said.

Mrs. Mills was out on the pavement, scooping at the air with her right arm. Gertie instinctively obeyed the order; Mr. Trew kept pace with her. The three entered the shop, and Mrs. Mills, with a touch of her heel, closed the door, went inside the tobacco counter, and, across it, spoke rapidly and vehemently, with the aid of emphatic gesture, for five minutes by the clock. Mr. Trew, disregarding rules of etiquette, sat down, whilst the two stood, and became greatly interested in the mechanism of a cigar-cutter.

"Who told you all this, aunt?" asked the girl calmly, when Mrs. Mills had finished.

"The lady customer who was here when you went out. Do you deny it? Of course, if it isn't correct that you've been seen walking about with a young swell, I've lost my temper for nothing."

"Girls will be girls," interposed Mr. Trew.

"Not in my house."

"It's all perfectly correct," announced Gertie.

Mrs. Mills looked around in a dazed way.

"Trew," she cried, "what's to be done?"

"You've had your say, old beauty," he remarked slowly. "Now let me and her go into the parlour and have some music—music of a different kind."

The girl hesitated, and looked through the window. He touched her shoulder. "I sh'd take it as a special favour."

He came out a few minutes later, and mentioned to Gertie's aunt that he had a message to deliver. The music within ceased; the lid of the pianoforte closed.

"Trew," she said.

"Queen of my heart."

"This isn't the only upset I've had. Who do you think it was in that ambulance cart this afternoon? I hopped across to have a look." Leaning over the counter, she whispered.

"That complicates matters, so far as she is concerned," he admitted. "I hoped he'd vanished for good. We shall want all the diplomacy that we've got stored away to deal with this."

CHAPTER II

Mr. Trew could scarcely be suspected of exceeding his instructions; he had, upon his return, given privately an account of the words used, with frequent use of the phrases, "I says to him," and "He says to me." But as evenings of the week went by, and other girls at Hilbert's, on leaving at the hour of seven, were met by courageous youths near the door, and by shyer lads at a more reticent spot (some of these took ambush in doorways, affecting to read cricket results in the evening paper), then Gertie Higham began to wonder whether the message had been communicated in the precise tone and manner that she had given it. The blue pinafored girls, stitching gold thread in the workroom at Hilbert's, cultivated little reserve, and when they had occasion to enter the office they sometimes told her of young men encountered (say) at a dance, of ardent protestations of love, faithful promises to meet again.

"And from that day to this," the accounts finished, "not so much as a sign of his lordship."

There was encouragement in the thought that he knew the number in Great Titchfield Street; was aware that she walked thence to Praed Street. And each evening on the way home a straw hat temporarily imposed upon her, a tall boyish figure and an eager method of walking deceived. At Praed Street, Mrs. Mills, noting that time had not been wasted on the journey, beamed approval and made much of her niece, telling her she was a good, sensible girl; one bound to get on in the world. Gertie did not leave again after her arrival, but turned out a room upstairs, and swept and dusted with extraordinary energy.

Good spirits increased at Great Titchfield Street when Friday came, and men at the looms above sang loudly; girls who had borrowed small sums were reminded by lenders that the moment for payment was close at hand. At the hour, wages were given through the pigeon-hole of the windows by Madame, with the assistance of Gertie, and the young women hung up pinafores, pinned hats, and flew off with the sums as though there was danger of a refund being demanded. When they had gone, Madame, dispirited by the paying out of money, said there was not now the profit in the business that there had been in her father's day, when you charged what you liked, and everybody paid willingly. To restore cheerfulness, the two faced each other at the sloping desks, and Madame dictated whilst Gertie took bills, headed "Hilbert's Military Accoutrement Manufacturers," and wrote the words, "To a/c rendered." Later, she left to Madame the task of locking up.

Near the print shop over the way, a tall young figure in a tweed suit marched from one unlighted lamp-post to another; the girl drew back to the staircase, snatching a space for consideration. The next moment she was crossing the street with the air of an art patron anxious to inspect before making a purchase.

"You gave me such a start," she declared, as a hand touched her shoulder lightly. "I'd begun to think you'd disappeared altogether. Where've you been hiding?"

"Do you mind very much," he asked, gazing down at her contentedly, "if I honour you with my company a part of the way?"

"No objection whatever. Hasn't it been a scorcher? Up there, what with the heat and the noise of the machines going, it's made my head ache."

"You won't care to go to a concert then. Shall we have a boat again in Regent's Park? We are both magnificent sailors."

"I'd rather be somewheres where we can talk."

"Why," he declared, "that is just what I should prefer. The similarity in our tastes is almost alarming."

"Primrose Hill is rather a nice open space."

"Sounds perfectly delightful," he agreed; "but I can't in the least guess where it is."

"I know my way about London," said Gertie Higham.

They walked along Oxford Street, the girl endeavouring to keep in step with him, and he attempting to keep in step with her; they appeared to decide near to Wells Street that it would be more convenient to fall back on individual methods. At the corner of Tottenham Court Road Gertie hailed a yellow omnibus which was on the point of starting; she skipped up the steps with a confidence that made the conductor's warning "'Old tight!" superfluous.

"You didn't mind my sending out that message the other evening?" Beginning the conversation breathlessly.

"I considered it kind of you to be so thoughtful."

"It wasn't exactly that. I didn't want a row with aunt. What did you think of Mr. Trew?"

"Do you know, it occurred to me that he looked rather like an omnibus driver."

"He is an omnibus driver."

"A relative?"

"Better than that—a friend. I s'pose you're somewhat particular about relations?"

The conductor came, and the girl had thought of other questions by the time fares to the Adelaide were paid. A man on the seat in front turned to ask her companion for a match; he handed over a silver box that bore a monogram. She begged permission, when it was given back, to look at the case.

"Which stands for the Christian name?"

"The H."

"And D. is for the surname then—H. D."

"Henry Douglass," he said.

"I like the sound of it," she declared. "What do you think the name of the forewoman at our place of business is?" She chattered on, and he listened attentively, as though the sound of her voice was all that mattered.

At the Adelaide they alighted, and, walking up the short hill, found Regent's Park Road; she explained the geography of the district, pointed out that away south it was all open country until you came to Marylebone Road. And was it not wonderful how fresh and bracing the air seemed up here, even on a summer's evening; you could easily imagine yourself miles and miles away from London. Did he care for the country? She did not. For one thing, the people there had such an odd way of speaking that it was a trouble to realize what they were driving at. She sometimes wondered whether they understood each other.

"You're letting me do all the talk," she remarked, as they took seats in the enclosed space at the top of the hill. Boys were playing on the slopes, punctuating the game with frequent disputes. A young couple seated near a tree attracted her notice; the girl's eyes were closed, head resting on the shoulder of the young man, who had an aspect of gloomy resignation.

"Sillies some people make of themselves, don't they?" she said.

"I suppose we are, most of us, ludicrous to other people."

"Do you laugh at me sometimes?"

"No, no," he said earnestly; "I like you too much to do that."

"You think you're a bit fond of me," she said, gazing ahead and speaking deliberately, "because I'm different from most of the girls you're in the habit of meeting, and my ways make a change for you. That's about all. You'd soon get tired of me and my manner if we saw much of each other. I know it won't last."

"I shall not trouble to contradict that," he remarked good-temperedly, "because I know you don't believe it yourself. Why, it would be absolutely splendid to be always with you."

Another couple walked by, breathless after the climb. Gertie, recognizing her friend Miss Radford, nodded; and that young lady, after a short scream of astonishment, gave a bow, and nudged her blushing companion as an instruction to imitate the example by raising his hat.

"I'm glad she's seen us," said Gertie. "Didn't the young fellow turn red?"

"He's a junior clerk in my office."

"What a score for me!" she cried exultantly. "I've a good mind to ask you now what you do for a living exactly, only that I'd rather find everything out bit by bit."

"You queer little person," he said affectionately. "Tell me instead about yourself. What is a day like at your place of business? Do you mind—it helps to concentrate my attention—if I hold your hand whilst you talk?"

"Why should I?" asked Gertie.

There could be no doubt, as she progressed with the description of Great Titchfield Street, that her mind was well occupied with the daily work; she gave the recital clearly and well, avoiding repetition and excluding any suggestion of monotony. Every moment of the hours there seemed to engage her interest. It was her duty to keep the books, and keep them straight; to answer the telephone, and sometimes make purchases of reels of gold thread and of leather. The looms and the netting machine were worked by men; the rest was done by girls. The forewoman was described, and her domestic troubles lightly sketched (Miss Rabbit's father backed horses, excepting when they came in first). Madame herself was spoken of in lowered respectful tones—partly because of her high position, partly because of shrewd and businesslike methods. Madame, it appeared, attributed any success she attained to the circumstance that she had steered clear of matrimony. Madame told the girls sometimes that you could wed yourself to business, or you could wed yourself to a man, but women who tried to do both found themselves punished for bigamy, sooner or later. Gertie was a favourite of Madame's; the main reason was, the girl thought, that—

"Shan't tell you!" she said, interrupting herself.

"Let me hear the worst," begged young Douglass cheerfully. "I have, just for the moment, the courage of a lion."

"Well, the reason is that she's under the impression I don't care much for—for anybody special."

"And is Madame correct in her sanguine anticipations?"

"She was. Until a month or so ago."

He took the other hand quickly.

"Let's move on," she recommended, rising sedately. "I don't want to be too late on pay night. Aunt will be thinking I've been knocked down and robbed of my purse. She's country-bred—Berkshire—and she says she doesn't trust Londoners." They went down the slope.

"Does she happen to know the town of Wallingford, I wonder?"

He declared, on receiving the answer, that nothing could be more fortunate; this was, indeed, pure luck. For he too was acquainted with Wallingford, and especially well he knew a village not far off: if he could but meet Gertie's aunt, here was a subject of mutual interest. Throwing away the serious manner that came intermittently, he challenged her to race him down to the Albert Road gate; and she went at her best speed, not discouraged by shouts from youngsters of "Go it, little 'un!" They arrived together at the gate, where Gertie had to rest for a few moments to regain breath. She pointed out that skirts hampered one; he admitted he ought to have given her fifty yards start. They took Regent's Park more demurely.

"When you get a colour," he said, "you look like a schoolgirl."

"As a matter of fact, I shan't see twenty again."

"Do you want to?"

"No," she replied candidly; "I'm as happy just now as ever I want to be. It'll always be something to look back upon."

"I wish," he said with earnestness, "that you wouldn't talk as though our friendship was only going to be temporary."

"We never know our luck," she remarked. "Aunt was saying only the other evening, 'Gertie,' she said— Now I've been and let you know my name."

He repeated it twice quietly to himself.

"Have you been fond of any one before this?" she asked. The girl had so many questions that her mind jumped from one topic to another.

"Oh yes," he answered. "When I was a schoolboy at Winchester I fell in love—deeply in love. She was a widow, and kept a confectioner's shop. Good shop, too."

"Nothing more serious than that?" He shook his head. "Glad I'm the first," she said. "And I wish my plan for getting you acquainted with aunt had come off the other night. It would have made it all seem more legal, somehow."

"We'll manage it," he promised. "Meanwhile, and always, don't forget that you are my dear sweetheart."

Miss Radford called at Praed Street, inquiring anxiously; and Mrs. Mills, summoning invention to her aid, said Gertie was not in. Mrs. Mills followed this up by mentioning that an occasional visit from Miss Radford could be tolerated, but it was not necessary for her to be always in and out of the place. Miss Radford, asserting that she never forced her company upon any one, swung out of the shop; and Mrs. Mills said to the cat that they did not want too many flighters about.

"Why, Mr. Bulpert!" With a quick change of manner to a newcomer. "This is a pleasant surprise. Mr. Trew was talking about you not two days ago."

The young man took the chair near the counter and, giving it a twirl, sat down heavily, and rested his chin on the back. "I'm putting on too much avoirdupois," he said gloomily. "Saturday, I had to get into evening dress, and it was as much as I could do to make the waistcoat buttons meet."

"You ought to take more exercise."

"What's the use of talking like that? If I take more exercise, I find myself with a bigger appetite, and then I'm worse off than ever." He dismissed the problem as insoluble. "Where's Gertie? I've got a new recitation that she'd very much like to hear. I place a certain value on her criticism."

"I'll call her down. And, Mr. Bulpert, I want you to be as nice and pleasant to her as you can. I had to talk rather sharply to her not many days ago; now I'd like to make it up. I'm bound to say she took it very well."

"You won't forget," he urged, "that I'm a man who can always get any amount of refined society. Sought after as I am for al fresco concerts and what not—"

"I know," agreed Mrs. Mills. "Only Gertie hasn't many friends, and I want her, just now, to make the most of 'em."

She called her niece, and Gertie came, turning the page of a book, entitled, "Hints for Gentlewomen." Gertie offered her hand to Bulpert, and remarked that he was growing stout; he advised her, with some vehemence, to take to glasses before her eyesight became further impaired. Mrs. Mills went back to the shop with a waggish caution against too much love-making. Bulpert, after shifting furniture, took up a position on the white hearthrug, and gave a stirring adventure in the life of a coastguardsman who saved from a wreck his wife and child. At the end, Bulpert mopped face, readjusted collar, and waited for congratulations.

"Did you make it up out your own head, Mr. Bulpert?"

"I did not make it up out of my own head," he said resentfully. "That isn't my line, and well you know it. It was written by a chap your cousin, Clarence Mills, introduced me to."

"Ask him to write it again. It seems to me a stupid piece. The wife's been away for ten years, and the baby is eighteen months old."

"That does require a slight alteration. But what about my rendering of it?"

"Overdone," answered Gertie. "If only you'd stand up and say them quietly, your pieces would go a lot better."

"But I've got to convey the meaning to the ordience."

"Give 'em credit for some intelligence. When the coastguardsman is going out to the wreck, it isn't necessary to wave your arms about like a windmill. You say he's swimming, and that's enough. And if a floating spar knocked him senseless before he got to the wreck, I don't believe he could take them both in his arms and swim back to the shore."

"It says he did in the poetry," contended Bulpert with warmth. "The whole fact of the matter is that you don't in the least know what you're talking about." A sound of voices came from the shop, and Gertie flushed. "Now it's no use your getting hot-tempered about it," he went on. "You speak your mind to me, and I'm entitled to speak my mind to you. What you suffer from is nothing more nor less than sheer ignorance. Imperfect education; that's what the complaint is called."

"Gertie!" A call from the shop.

"Yes, aunt."

"Do come here just a moment. Here's the strangest coincidence I ever came across." Gertie obeyed with signs of nervousness. "This young gentleman tells me that he knows Ewelme, and he's actually been inside the house where I was born!"

"How do you do?" said Gertie.

"And he's going down there again shortly," went on Mrs. Mills with animation, "and he means to bring me back some roses from the garden. Isn't it good of him?"

"Your daughter is fond of flowers?"

"She's only my niece," explained Mrs. Mills volubly. "Her mother kicked the bucket some years ago, and her father—What's Wallingford like now, sir? I've said over and over again that I'd one day take the Great Western to go and have a look and see what alterations had been made. But," regretfully, "it's never been anything more than talk. I'd like Gertie to see the place though, so that she could tell whether it comes up to my description."

He seemed inclined to make an impetuous offer, but a brief shake of the girl's head arrested him. A boy entered and asked for an evening newspaper, and Gertie attended to the transaction.

"By the bye," turning to the stationery counter, "I want one or two magazines." Their heads came closely together as a selection was being made; she whispered a caution not to stay too long. In a louder voice, Gertie announced that the total cost was two shillings and sixpence. Mrs. Mills beamed across from the tobacco counter, and asked whether he knew who was keeping "The Lamb"; Henry Douglass could not supply the information, but guaranteed to obtain particulars, and bring them to Praed Street. Mrs. Mills declared herself ashamed to give so much trouble.

"Are you in business, sir, may I ask?"

"I am, in a very small way, an architect."

"Really?" said Gertie interestedly.

"But," said Mrs. Mills, "you're not wearing a white tie!"

"She's thinking of an archbishop," remarked Bulpert, coming forward. "I'm pleased to make your acquaintance, sir. Daresay you know me by name." He found a card in his letter-case, and Henry took it near the light to examine the wording.

"'Fred W. Bulpert,'" he read. "'Society Entertainer and Elocutionist.'"

"That's in the evenings, of course," said Bulpert. "By day, I'm in the West Central district. Post Office, to tell you the truth. I'll trouble you for the card back, because I'm running somewhat short of them. And if you should be arranging a concert at any time, either for your own benefit or any body else's, you might bear me in mind. F. W. B. is a great draw, if I may say so, because, you see, a lot of people have heard him before."

The customer asked whether there was an underground station near; Mrs. Mills instructed Gertie to walk along with the young gentleman, and to point out the building. As they left, she urged Henry not to forget his promise concerning the roses.

"Nice, quiet-spoken lad," she commented. "I wish Gertie would take up with some one like him, or even you, and forget all about that society young man she's been seen strolling with."

"I hadn't heard about that," said Bulpert seriously. "What are the solid facts of the matter? Why am I kept in the dark about everything?"

CHAPTER III

Mr. Trew, off duty, and carrying his whip, came to Praed Street late on a Saturday night, and his look of anxiety disappeared at once when he saw that Mrs. Mills and her niece were on excellent terms with each other. He explained that there was no time to spare, because his old landlady had a hot supper ready, and it was not wise, on these occasions, to keep her or the meal waiting. He delivered his news. Pleasant, elderly gent on the front seat started conversation by talking about prison life, and Trew gave some particulars of a case with which he was acquainted. One subject leading to another, the gent said, as the omnibus was crossing Oxford Street, "Driver, do you ever go to the Zoological Gardens on a Sunday afternoon?" and thereupon handed over the two tickets, expressing a hope that the visit would be enjoyed by the other and his wife.

"And me being nothing more than a lonely bachelor," said Trew, "I thought perhaps the little missy here might favour me with her company."

"It'll do her the world of good," declared Mrs. Mills.

They met the next day near the West Entrance at half-past three. Mr. Trew, arriving early, had been listening to oratory at different groups, and he mentioned to Gertie that in his opinion some of the speakers might well be transferred to the Gardens, and kept in a cage; what he failed to understand was why people could not set to and make the best of the world, instead of pretending it was all bad. They went through the turnstiles, and divided attention between animals and visitors; the former could be identified with the help of labels. Mr. Trew said, in regard to the people, that it was difficult to tell which were housemaids, and which were ladies of title.

"Oddly enough," remarked Gertie, "I was intending to be here this afternoon, in any case."

"Trust me," he said, self-reproach fully, "for coming in second. Never actually won a race in my life yet. Is it the same young feller?"

"I'm not one to chop and change."

"When we run across him, I'll make myself scarce."

"You'll do nothing of the kind, Mr. Trew."

He pointed out, in the crocodile house, one or two regular customers of the Baker Street to Victoria route, and when they recognized him he became purple with content. A short youth was making notes near a tank in the corner. Mr. Trew, nudging Gertie, went to him and, in a gruff voice, asked what the deuce he was doing there; the youth turned to give a retort.

"I've got your young lady cousin with me," explained Mr. Trew. "Come along, and help with the task of looking after her."

Clarence Mills was pleased to meet Gertie, and, as the three went towards the red-bricked lions' house, mentioned that he proposed to write a dialogue sketch of the Zoo; up to the present little worth recording had been overheard, and he expected he would, as usual, be compelled to invent the conversations.

"I read all of yours, Clarence, that appear in the newspapers," said Gertie.

"That doesn't take up a great deal of your time," he remarked.

"But you're getting on, aren't you?"

"I think of going in for the boot-black business," he said. "I believe I could make a reputation there."

"Don't you go losing 'eart," advised Mr. Trew. "I shouldn't be in the position I occupy now if I hadn't made up my mind, from the start, not to get low-spirited. If any disappointments come your way, simply laugh at 'em. They can stand anything but that. Who is this I see on the far horizon?"

"Don't let him catch sight of us just yet," begged the girl apprehensively. "He seems to have ladies with him."

Henry's companions entered the house, as the roaring within became insistent, and he looked up and down eagerly. Gertie gave a whistle.

"You and I have met before," he said smilingly to Mr. Trew.

"I was a Boy Messenger then, sir."

Gertie introduced her cousin with a touch of pride.

"I am trying to think," said Clarence, "where I saw your name to-day."

"Haven't made a name yet," remarked Henry. "Only been at it for about eighteen months. I say! We don't want to go into that enormous crowd. We'll stroll round and see how the penguins are getting on. They sometimes look as though they were thinking of giving me a commission to draw up plans for new Law Courts."

At one of the open windows the two ladies were standing, watching over many heads the high tea that was being served to the impatient animals. The younger one happened to turn as Gertie and her friends went by; she raised her eyebrows.

"Everybody one knows appears to be here," said Henry Douglass. "I wish you had agreed instead to run out with me from Baker Street Station into the country."

"Can't do that yet," she answered definitely. "Not until we know each other a great deal better."

"Your rules of conduct are precise."

"You'll like me all the better later on," said Gertie, "because of that. Always supposing," she continued, "that you do go on liking me."

"So far as I can gather," he remarked good-temperedly, "I am persona grata now at Praed Street."

"I don't know what that means," she said; "but aunt has quite taken to you. Just look at this! Isn't it extr'ordinary?—Clarence," she called over her shoulder to her cousin, "here is most likely where you saw the name this afternoon."

She examined the inscription framed on the bars. "Presented to the Society by Sir Mark Douglass."

"No," said Clarence Mills. "That wasn't it. My sluggish memory will arouse presently, and then I shall be able to exhibit signs of intelligence."

They were looking down from the terrace at the white bear in his pit, when a high voice came above the moderate tones of the crowd; Henry took Gertie's arm, and began to talk rapidly of Nansen and the North Pole, but this did not prevent her from glancing over her shoulder. The people gave way to the owner of the insistent voice, and she, after inspection through pince-nez, made bitter complaint of the clumsiness of the bear, his murky appearance, the serious consequences of indiscriminate feeding. Henry endeavoured to detach the members of his party, but they appeared enthralled by the commanding tones.

"I thought we should meet again," said the younger woman, addressing Henry.

"Miss Loriner," he said to Gertie, with signs of reluctance. "A friend of my sister-in-law."

"I am Lady Douglass's companion," remarked Miss Loriner.

"She seems ratty about something," said Gertie.

"She has what they call the critical faculty," mentioned the other, with a twinkle of the eye. "I happen to be aware of the fact."

Lady Douglass was looking around with the air of one searching for fresh subjects; Henry led Gertie to her, and made the introductions. Lady Douglass expressed the view that the Gardens were horribly tiring, regretted her ill-luck in visiting on a crowded afternoon. "But no misfortune," she added wearily, "seems to escape me!"

It was not until they descended the steps that the group had an opportunity for forming itself. Miss Loriner, recognizing the girl's perturbation of mind, took her ahead, thus foiling the intentions of Lady Douglass; they could hear her talking of literature to Clarence Mills in a patronizing way. Gertie's cousin said resolutely, "But George Meredith never wrote a poem with that title. You are thinking of Owen Meredith." Lady Douglass answered, with pride, that she never troubled to remember the names of authors.

"Clarence is standing up to her," remarked Gertie.

"She gets so little contradiction," said Miss Loriner, "that it will have all the charm of novelty. I daren't do it, of course."

"You're thinking of your bread and butter."

"That's about all I should have to eat if I lost this berth."

"Wouldn't care for the job myself."

"I can't do anything else," explained Miss Loriner. "Did you say your cousin was a journalist? I wish I could do something like that. I want to write a novel, badly."

"That's probably how you would write it. Why, even Clarence is finding some trouble over the job. And he's got a brain."

"I suppose that is an advantage," admitted the other serenely. "How long have you known Mr. Douglass?"

"Her husband must get precious tired of the sound of her voice."

"He does. He goes away a good deal. The war in South Africa was a Godsend to him. Just now he is out somewhere—I forget where. How long have you—"

"Any youngsters?"

"There are no children."

Gertie glanced back at Lady Douglass in a more friendly way. Clarence had been dropped owing, apparently, to want of sympathy, and Trew was selected as one more likely to agree with arguments.

"Mr. Douglass's mother is in town," mentioned Miss Loriner, "but she is resting this afternoon."

"I wasn't aware he had a mother."

"Oh!" With illumination. "Then you haven't known him long. They are very fond of each other. She is a dear soul. When matters go wrong down at Ewelme, it is old Mrs. Douglass who puts everything right."

They were separated by a child who had been startled by a look from an amiable dromedary. Henry came forward.

"I am going to ask my sister-in-law," he said deliberately, "to invite you down to Morden Place. Thank her, won't you?"

"I'll thank her," replied Gertie, "but I shan't accept the invitation."

"I'd see that she was civil to you."

"And I shall see," said the girl obstinately, "that she doesn't get many chances of being anything else. I'd no idea you had swell relatives; otherwise I'd never have gone on with it."

He went back disappointedly, and Mr. Trew, making his escape with every sign of relief, told Gertie that, with what he might term a vast and considerable experience of womankind (including one specimen who, in May of '99, gave him advice on the task of driving horses through London streets), this particular one was, he declared, the limit. He described himself as feeling bruised, black and blue, all over. Without wishing to interfere in matters which did not concern him, he ventured to suggest that Gertie might possibly be fortunate in her young man, but she could scarcely claim to be called lucky in her young man's relations.

"I'm going to chuck it," she replied desperately. "Chuck it altogether. You were correct in what you said, that Sunday night, about distances, and I was wrong."

Mr. Trew, flustered by this instant agreement, began to hedge. He did not pretend, he said, to be always right; he could recollect many occasions when he had been considerably wide of the mark. In fact, a bigger blunderhead, excepting in regard to certain matters, of which this was not one, probably did not exist. Trew begged to point out that the middle-aged party walking along behind them was, after all, only one middle-aged party, and there was no reason to assume that she could knock out every opponent she encountered. At the finish of his argument, Trew urged his young companion to put on the gloves, and show what she could do.

"Think I had better not," she said, less definitely. "I shan't like feeling myself beaten, but it's wiser to do that now than to leave it till later."

Mr. Trew became reproachful, almost sarcastic. This, then, was the stuff that his little friend, niece of his old friend, was made of, was it? Crumpling up at the first signs of opposition; stepping out of the ring directly her opponent held up fists! If Gertie represented the young woman of to-day, give Mr. Trew the young woman of thirty years ago. He had changed his mind recently on an important subject—a thing he rarely did—and half decided to extend the power of voting to the other sex, but the present case induced him to believe first thoughts were best.

"I'll have another go then," announced Gertie Higham; "but I don't guarantee I shall win."

"If I hadn't rather a lot of money out just now," he declared encouragingly, "I'd put every penny of it on you."

They stopped near to the semicircular cage where the condors, in evening dress and white boa around the neck, surveyed the garden with the aloof manner of the higher aristocracy. Gertie waited for an advance; this did not come. Miss Loriner, at the command of Lady Douglass, furnished the hour, and a scream of dismay was given, followed by the issuing of orders. Henry must conduct them out of this dreadful Park; Henry must find a hansom with a reliable horse, and a driver of good reputation. Also Henry must come on to see his mother, and take her on to a tea appointment at Cadogan Gardens, thus saving trouble to Lady Douglass, who was really so fagged and wearied by this exhausting afternoon that rest, in a partially darkened room, was nothing short of imperative.

"Yes," said Gertie, answering Henry's questioning look; "you go!"

Lady Douglass remembered to give a word of farewell when she was a distance of about ten yards away. "So pleased to have met you!" she said casually. Henry, near the gates, turned and waved his hand, and Gertie responded cheerfully.

"Now I want to scream!" she said.

Clarence Mills declared his intention of providing tea, and Trew admitted a cup or so would not be likely to prove injurious to the system; might, indeed, have a soothing effect on the mind. They found an enamelled table on the lawn, and directly Gertie took the handle of the teapot she was able to announce that she felt considerably improved in temper. Her cousin gave an imitation of Lady Douglass's speech and manner, and Gertie imitated the imitation. Mr. Trew had a difficulty in deciding which was the more admirable, but asserted either was to be preferred to the original, and during the progress of the shilling meal they affected to be distinguished members of society, to the great astonishment of folk at neighbouring tables, and to the diversion of an interested waiter. Completely restored now to her normal mood, Gertie mentioned a number of alert repartees which she would have made if Henry's sister-in-law had given suitable openings.

"I suppose," remarked Mr. Trew, emptying his cup by giving it a jerk over his shoulder, "that, after all, she isn't nearly so bad as she's painted. She certainly did look to me somewhat made-up; it's a custom amongst her set, I believe. Often wonder whether it takes anybody in."

"He said she was going to invite me to her house in the country, but she didn't. Wouldn't mind meeting Henry's mother, just once, to find out what she is like."

"It was something on the tape," mentioned her cousin, again endeavouring to arouse memory. "That was where I saw the name. If you two care to come along to my club, I'll run in, and make sure."

"We can get a Waterloo omnibus from the York and Albany corner," said Mr. Trew.

He warned them, in ascending the steps, that he was going to have a rare lark with the driver, whose face, it appeared, was new on the road. They took seats in front, and Mr. Trew, adopting a rustic accent, inquired of the driver whether the canal below represented the river Thames; in regard to Trinity Church, near Portland Road Station, he asked if he was right in assuming this to be St. Paul's; at Peter Robinson's he put another question, and, information given, demanded whether Oxford Circus was being run by Barnum. These and other inquiries were courteously replied to; and when the three alighted near the fountain and Trew, looking up, thanked the new driver for his kindness, the driver said, "Ta-ta, old True till Death," whipping the omnibus on the near side to call the conductor's attention to an approaching customer.

Mr. Trew, depressed by the failure of his elaborate scheme, walked behind the young people, grumbling self-reproachfully. "Him recognizing me all along, and calling me by my nickname at the finish!"

Clarence Mills ran up the staircase of his club, and the two walked inside the railings of the square, inspected the bust of Shakespeare at the centre. A few people were sitting about. The palatial houses of amusement on the northern and the western side enjoyed their day of rest, but gave hints of startling attractions for the coming week. Mr. Trew considered Shakespeare a well-meaning writer, but somewhat old fashioned in methods, and was surprised to find that Gertie had thoroughly enjoyed "The Tempest" at His Majesty's.

"Was you alone?"

"No. Mr. Douglass took me."

"That accounts for it," he said knowingly.

Clarence Mills came looking for them with anxiety. The two hurried forward and met him at the gate; his forehead remained contracted.

"Her husband's yacht," he announced, "has been seized by natives. All on board put to death." They gazed at each other.

"So that turns her," remarked Trew slowly, "into a widow woman. There's no family, as I understand; consequently, it makes a bit of diff'rence to Gertie's young man."

The girl sighed.

"I'm sorry for her," she said. "Very sorry indeed. And it means that my path won't be none the easier!"

CHAPTER IV

Madame Hilbert and the forewoman in Great Titchfield Street consulted each other only when crises occurred; the girls knew that if Madame came to the doorway, saying, "Miss Rabbit, just half a second, please," and the forewoman was absent for half an hour, then some matter of supreme importance was being discussed. The establishment was in close touch with the military service at home and abroad, and the best stroke good fortune could make in favour of Hilbert's was to arrange a stately ceremonial in India, some alteration in the dress of officers, or anything that made uniforms necessary. The girls' workroom, even at ordinary times, presented an aspect of enormous wealth, with everywhere a display of gold—loose threads of it on the tables, collected threads being sewn on foundations, epaulettes in course of making, heavy dependent nuggets hung upon scarves. Gold floated in the air, and when the sun came through the windows it all looked as though one could play the conjurer, and perform the enchanting trick of making a dash with the hand and secure sovereigns. Many of the girls wore glasses because continued attention to the glistening colours affected the eyes; sometimes a worker became pale of features, anaemic and depressed, and had to hurry off to the sea-side, and Miss Rabbit referred to this as an act of Providence. For the most part, the girls were healthy and cheerful, and they had the encouragement of good wages. Miss Rabbit, it was reported, took home every Saturday two pounds ten shillings; the very youngest assistant made twelve shillings a week.

"I do hope," said Madame, at a special private conference, "it doesn't mean she's taking up religion." The forewoman shook her head. "I've known cases in my time where it's come on suddenly, and it's thrown a girl clean off her balance. If it isn't religion it must be love. Love has just about the same effect with some of us. Have you ever been gone on any one, Miss Rabbit?"

"Only to a very moderate extent," replied the forewoman precisely. "And it's such a long while ago, Madame, that I've nearly forgot all about it."

"I don't like to see one of my girls turn like this all at once," said Madame with anxiety. "Moreover, she's the handy one in the business. There's nothing she doesn't know about the work, and little she can't do. If anything happened to you, I've always had the idea of putting her in your position."

Miss Rabbit's features twitched; she corrected the slip at once by assuming a look of cordial agreement. "You always know the right thing to do, Madame," she murmured reverently.

"How'd it be to call her in, and both of us have a talk to her, and find out whether she's got anything on her mind?"

"That's a splendid notion," admitted Miss Rabbit with enthusiasm. "Or shall I have a quiet chat with her first, and pave the way, so to speak?"

"I wish you would," said Madame. "You're not particularly clever, but I believe you've got a kind heart."

The forewoman that evening, whilst the girls were washing and sharing the brush and comb, and complaining that hair came out by the handful, entered the office; announcing the occasion as her birthday, she asked Miss Higham to leave books, and assist in celebrating the event by taking with her a cup of chocolate. Gertie wanted to reach home early in order to see whether an expected letter had arrived, but the invitation suggested a rare compliment, and, with a stipulation arranging that the hospitality should not exceed the space of twenty minutes, she accepted. In an A.B.C. shop at the corner, later, Gertie raised her large cup and wished Miss Rabbit many happy returns. Her eyes wandered rather eagerly about the crowded tables; the inspection over, she sighed.

"Wonder if I can trust you, dear," said Miss Rabbit, resting elbows. "I've been so often taken in over friendships with people that I suppose I'm more cautious than most. But there's a look about you— perhaps, though, I'd better keep on the safe side."

"I'm not one to chatter."

"I know, I know. That's why I've always took to you specially." Again Miss Rabbit stopped. She stirred her cup of chocolate slowly.

"If it's good news," advised Gertie, "tell me. I can do with some just now. If it's not, keep it to yourself."

"It's rather serious news, and that's why I think you ought to be told. First of all, you must promise me, on your soul and honour, not to breathe a word of it to anybody. Above all, not to Madame."

"I promise," she said.

"Very well then"—with a satisfied air—"it's like this." She leaned across the marble table. "Our show is going to burst up."

The dramatic announcement over, and the appropriate ejaculation, the correct look of amazement and despair given. Miss Rabbit warmed to her task, and became voluble; at each new paragraph of her discourse she exacted a fresh guarantee that the information would go no further, that the bond of absolute secrecy should be respected. Once, she felt it necessary to say that if the other communicated a single word of the confidences to any third party, she, Miss Rabbit, would feel it her duty to haunt Miss Higham to the last hour of her life. Put briefly, the news came to this. That Madame was in financial difficulties; that her name and address might be found in the bankruptcy list any coming Wednesday or Saturday; that no one was likely to be stupid enough to take over the business; that the members of the staff, men and girls, would find themselves turned out into a cold, hard world. The drawback of being connected with a business of a special nature like theirs was that there existed but few of a similar nature, and these were already fully supplied with assistants. Miss Rabbit herself intended to look out for another berth ere the market became swamped by many applications; with piety, she called attention to a well-known text which said, "Go thou and do likewise." Outside the A.B.C. shop, Miss Rabbit, in extorting thanks for her generous behaviour, demanded, once more, a promise.

"Say it after me," she ordered. "'I will never utter a single syllable of all this to a solitary living soul.'" Her instructions complied with, she remarked that a great load was now taken from her mind, and asked Gertie for advice on the point whether to go home by omnibus or Tube railway.

The girl arrived at Praed Street after a brisk walk that was intended to detach the mind from disturbing incident. In the broad thoroughfare of Portland Place (which looked as though it started with the idea of being a long, important roadway to the north, and became suddenly reminded, to its great astonishment, that Regent's Park barred the way) she had glanced up at the large houses, and wished she lived in one; in that case she would receive Henry Douglass, at the end of the silence that had come since the last meeting, and after listening to him, reject his advances haughtily. That was the phrase. Reject his advances haughtily. She had read it more than once in the literature which attracted her in the days before Henry. Since she had known him, a course of reading, adopted at his suggestion, took her away from the more flowery and romantic pages, but in the old serial stories the folk had nothing to do but to make love to each other, with intervals for meals and rest; they were not restricted to evening hours; the whole day was at their service. And certainly the ladies never found themselves burdened with the anxiety of losing a weekly wage, in Great Titchfield Street, and the prospect of difficulty in finding one to replace it.

"I'm home, aunt," she announced, entering the shop.

"So I see," remarked Mrs. Mills. Two customers were being served at the newspaper counter, and two were waiting on the tobacco side. Gertie attended to the orders for cigarettes; the shop cleared.

"Is there a letter for me?" she asked.

Mrs. Mills shook her head curtly.

"Has—has any one called?"

"Now, let me think." Her aunt deliberated carefully in the manner of a conscientious witness impressed by the taking of the oath. "Yes, Miss Radford looked in and went again. Left word that she wanted you to go with her for an outing next Saturday afternoon. Said she wanted a breath of fresh air. Mr. Trew is inside—and that reminds me, I've got something to say to him. Wait here, like a dear, and look after the shop." Mrs. Mills closed the door carefully behind her as she went into the parlour.

"So, Mr. Trew, I packed him off about his business," she said, obviously continuing a half-finished recital. "I said, 'She asked me to tell you that she thought it better for both parties that you and her shouldn't see each other again.' Don't blame me, do you?"

Mr. Trew rubbed his chin with the knuckle of a finger and remarked that, by rights, he ought to have a shave.

"I stopped his two letters when they came," went on Mrs. Mills. "Many a woman in my position would have been curious enough to open them; I didn't. I simply put them in a drawer where they can be found when the trouble's all over. No one can blame me for that, surely."

Mr. Trew mentioned that it was a rummy world, and the methods adopted by the people living in it did not make it the less rummy.

"I see what you mean," she said aggrievedly. "You think I've gone too far. But you yourself admitted at the start, when she was meeting that other young gentleman, that high and low never mixed well. And when I heard that this one was likely to come into property, I made up my mind to take the bull by the horns. What's that you say? Speak out, if you've got anything in your head."

"When you take the bull by the horns," said Trew, advancing to the white hearthrug, "what happens is a toss up. I can't tell you yet whether you've done right or whether you've done wrong; but if you put the question to me a 'underd years hence, I shall be able to answer you. What's pretty clear to me is that you're fond of her, and I'm fond of her, and all we want is to see her comfor'ble and happy. Whether you're taking the right track to gain that object is more than I can say. Personally, I shouldn't care to go so far as you've gone."

"That's because you're a coward."

"Delight of my juvenile heart," said Mr. Trew, "it's quite likely you've hit on precisely the right explanation. Only thing is, it seems to me somewhat rough on the little missy."

Miss Radford was studying the arrival of trains list at Paddington in order to ascertain from which platform the 1.20 p.m. started; she had assumed the slightly demented appearance that so many take when they enter a railway station. Turning from the poster distractedly, she clutched at the arm of a sailor, and was putting to him agitated inquiries concerning the Great Western service when Gertie Higham interposed, and released the naval man from a duty for which he was not adequately equipped. Firmly and resolutely she conducted Miss Radford to the correct platform, where they found seats in a compartment; and Miss Radford in vain tried to remember whether it was that sitting facing the engine or sitting with her back to the engine gave her a headache. Gertie had obtained the tickets, and Miss Radford wanted hers; Gertie retained possession. On the question of finance, she said a settlement could be arranged when the outing was over. Other passengers entered, including two lads, who set at once on the work of studying scientific books; Miss Radford, changing her manner, dropped her parasol as the train started, and one of the youths picked it up, without disengaging his attention from the volume, and handed it to her.

"Thanks awfully," she said, in refined and slightly languid tones; "I am such a clumsy creature"—partly addressing her friend, but mainly speaking to the entire compartment. "Really, I seem quite lost without my maid to look after me."

"You managed to get away from the shop in good time," remarked Gertie.

"What an irritating girl you are, to be sure!" whispered Miss Radford aggrievedly. "No help at all when I'm trying to make a good impression. Wish now I hadn't asked you to come along with me; I only did it because I couldn't get any one else. What's become of that young swell I saw you with on Primrose Hill?"

"I really don't know."

Miss Radford spoke complacently of her intense love of the country and keen anticipation of the joy to be found at Burnham Beeches, and when the train stopped at Slough the compartment mentioned to her that this was where she ought to alight. Gertie, interposing, said that they were, in reality, going further. On Miss Radford asking, in astonished tones, "Whatever for?" she received information that the desire was to get well away from the crowd. The two, changing at a junction, found a small train on another platform that had but a single line; Miss Radford took the precaution of inquiring of the engine-driver whether he considered it safe. The two lads crossed the bridge, and, to her intense annoyance, entered a smoking-compartment.

"I daresay, perhaps"—recovering from this blow—"that we shall manage to run across some others before the day's out."

"Hope not."

"Well, upon my word," declared the astonished Miss Radford, "you grow more and more peculiar every day!"

They discovered themselves, immediately after leaving the station yard, in an old-fashioned town with large houses close to the brick pavement; cyclists raced along the narrow roadway, and folk carried baskets in the direction of the river. Gertie stopped to put an inquiry to a policeman, and declined to satisfy her companion's curiosity either in regard to the question or to the answer. Turning to the right, they came to a market-place and a town hall, and, amongst the small shops, one that they noted as a suitable place for tea. The sun was warm, and folk were shopping with suitable deliberation; dogcarts stood outside the principal establishments, motor cars brought up new supplies of clients. Gertie appeared greatly interested in the occupants of these conveyances; some of the ladies were so well protected from dust that identification would not have been easy. Miss Radford mentioned that she had not seen so many funny figures about since the fifth of November of the previous year.

"Where are we off to now?" she demanded.

"A good long walk."

"Not me!" replied Miss Radford with determination. "I've got new shoes on. You leave me somewhere with a magazine to read, and go off on your own, and come back when you're tired."

"You won't be lonely?"

"I can always find a pleasure," said Gertie's friend haughtily, "in my own company."

The riverside, Miss Radford decided, was a suitable spot for rest; she could sit there and, in the intervals of application to literature of the day, watch young men hiring boats and setting out to Shillingford or Cholsey. So Gertie Higham started out across the bridge and walked alone through a village where every shop sold everything, where the police station was a homely, comfortable cottage, and children played on wide grass borders of the road. At the cross-roads she went to the left; an avenue of trees gave a shade that was welcome. The colour came to her face as she strode along briskly, and this was not entirely due to hurry or to the rays of the afternoon sun. Once or twice she almost stopped, as though considering the advisability of returning.

An ivy-covered house stood at the side of iron gates, and Gertie watched it as she approached. An elderly man was clipping hedges; he arrested his work, with an evident hope that conversation would occur.

"No, young 'ooman," he said, "that ent where her ladyship lives. That's only the gate lodge what you're looking at. A good ha'f-mile 'fore you come the house itself. Do you know her, may I inquire?"

"We've met in London."

"Well"—slowly, and making the most of the opportunity—"she ent pleased to see many of her visitors, if all I hear is true; but no doubt she'd be gratified to see you. I'm only a new-comer hereabouts, so to speak, but—" He shook his head thoughtfully, and, taking off his hat, readjusted the cabbage leaf that lined it. "I don't blame Sir Mark for going off and getting killed. After all, it ent as though she were left chargeable to the parish, as you may say."

"She is quite well to do, I suppose?"

"Plenty of money about, as me and you would rackon it. I understand she complains of not having enough—but there, some people are never satisfied. Going to give a party next week," he added confidentially. "Not a great turn-out, because they're all in black, so to speak. So fur as I can gain from the local newspaper—"

"You say it's half a mile up to the house?"

"You can't very well miss it if you foller your nose," said the old man, hurt by the interruption.

Through the iron gates Gertie saw two figures coming around the curve of the gravelled carriage-way; she took ambush hurriedly near to an oak tree. Henry's voice could be heard, with an occasional remark from Miss Loriner. "And if I promise to worship you all my life," Henry was saying, "will you then give me my heart's desire?" His companion did not reply; he repeated the last words. "You must first," she said, "make a name in the world, and show yourself worthy of a woman's love." They turned as they reached the gates, and when Henry next spoke his remarks did not reach the girl near the oak tree.

"And haven't you been a time!" complained Miss Radford. "Over a hower altogether, according to my watch. And I'm simply dying for a cup of tea. There's only been one young gentleman who waved his hand to me; I was so cross that I didn't wave back. Whatever are you dodging up to now?"

"I'm going to hire a boat," said Gertie, "and take you out on the river."

"You can't row."

"Some one learnt me—taught me on the lake in Regent's Park."

Miss Radford declared, on the journey home, that she envied her friend's good spirits; in her own case, she always found that if she became more than ordinarily cheerful she inevitably paid for it by subsequent depression. Gertie recommended her to adopt the method of not magnifying grievances; if you wanted to view trouble, you could take opera-glasses, but you should be careful to hold them the wrong way round. The studious youths entered the compartment at Goring, their books now put away in pockets, and similarly cheered by exercise; one, seated opposite Gertie, touched her foot with his shoe at Pangbourne, and she took no notice. When he did this again at Tilehurst, she came down heavily upon his toes, and gave, for her clumsiness, an apologetic word that he accepted sulkily. Near to Paddington, Miss Radford mentioned that, in her opinion, men were most frightfully stupid, and to her surprise Gertie agreed.

Gertie Higham relieved her aunt from duty in the shop, and a letter brought by the postman at nine o'clock was handed over the counter to her direct; the official recommended her to accept the offer, and put the young gentleman out of his misery. The communication was written in a large hand, about twelve words to a page, and liberally underlined. Printed in the corner were a telegraphic address, a telephone number, directions concerning nearest railway station. For heading, Morden Place, Ewelme.

"DEAR MISS HIGHAM,—We shall be so glad if you can pay us a visit on Friday next and stay over for the week-end. Dear Henry is particularly anxious that you should be here on Saturday evening.

"What a wonderful summer we are having!!!—Yours sincerely,

"MYRA DOUGLASS."

The girl found a sheet of the best notepaper on the shelves, and wrote at once.

"DEAR LADY DOUGLASS,—I shall not be able to come to you next Friday. I am rather busy.

"It is indeed a capital summer. I am enjoying it.—Yours sincerely,

"GERTRUDE HIGHAM."

CHAPTER V

An easy matter to obtain a full list of other manufacturers in the same line of business, and when Madame entrusted her with important errands,—

"I'm sending you, my dear, because I know I can rely upon you!"

—Then advantage was taken of the opportunity to skip up a staircase and, opening a door that had the word "Inquiries" painted upon it, set upon the task of routing the defence, to obtain an interview with some responsible individual. Usually the answer was that no vacancy existed, but this did not prevent a brief cross-examination. Why was she leaving Great Titchfield Street, and was it because there did not exist a sufficient amount of work, and had Hilbert's secured any important contracts lately, and had the firm any special work in view? To which questions Miss Higham replied with caution and reserve, so that frequently the responsible individual came out of his office, walking with her down the stairs in the endeavour to obtain useful information. As a rule, the discussion ended with a command that she should look in again when it chanced she was passing by. At Great Titchfield Street, when Miss Rabbit and Gertie happened to be, for the moment, alone, the forewoman begged her in a low, confidential whisper not to put off till to-morrow anything she could do to-day, adding that procrastination was the thief of time.

"The fact is," said Miss Rabbit, with a burst of private candour, "I don't care what happens so long as you are safe. Very strange, isn't it, dear?"

It seemed to the perplexed girl, at this period, that life was made up of incidents which could not be spoken about freely. There was no one with whom she could share the knowledge acquired at Wallingford; that had to be endured alone. At Praed Street she found her aunt gazing at her curiously, sometimes beginning a sentence, and stopping, as one fearful of trespassing on prohibited ground. When Mr. Trew called, he and Mrs. Mills conferred in undertones, breaking off when the girl came near, and speaking, in an unconvincing way, of an interesting murder in South London; Trew thought the police could find the missing man if they only went the right way about it. Great Titchfield Street, from eight o'clock in the morning till nearly eight at night, appeared to be enveloped in a dense fog, with Madame showing none of the distraction of mind natural to one on the edge of a financial crisis, and Bunny conveying friendliness by nods and furtive winks; the girls, as always, chattered freely of their small romances, not concealing their derisive attitude towards young men, excepting as means of escort and paymasters where sweets and tram-tickets were involved; any slackening of attention in these details, and dark hints were given of an intention of giving the sack. Listening, Gertie came to the conclusion that her own case was unique, in that she had allowed Henry Douglass to assume the position of autocrat. One of the men who worked the netting machine spoke to her exultantly of wisdom in managing his wife; the method adopted was, it seemed, to contradict every blessed thing she said.

On the top of all this comes Frederick Bulpert, encountered near Queen's Hall one evening at five minutes to eight, trying to make up his mind whether to spend a shilling on a promenade concert or to disburse the money on a steak—Bulpert very glad to meet Gertie, because he has something to say to her that he cannot speak of to any one else; something which must be regarded (says Frederick) as strictly entre nous. A spot of rain, and the stout young man says with a reckless air, "Oh, come on in!" and Gertie agrees to accompany him, with two provisions: first, that she shall be allowed to pay for herself; second (because aunt has a new trick of requiring every minute between Great Titchfield Street and Praed Street to be accounted for), that Frederick will see her home later to the shop. Gertie thinks a dose of music will do her as much good as anything.

"I don't claim," he admits, "to have an over and above savage breast, but I must confess it soothes me at times."

They are in time to take up position near the fountain in the centre of the promenade, to join in the welcome given to the leading men of the orchestra, to swell the applause offered to the conductor, to sing—this being the opening night—the National Anthem. Frederick takes what he calls seconds; neighbours misunderstand it for an expression of disloyalty. Then the programme starts. Frederick Bulpert, new silk hat at back of head, and arms folded, listens to the "William Tell" overture, Handel's "Largo," and the suite from "Peer Gynt" with the frown of a man not to be taken in and unwilling to be influenced by the approbation exhibited by people round him. A song follows, and he remarks to Gertie that a recitation would be more in keeping with the style of the entertainment. A violin solo with a melody that cries softly about love, the love of two people, with anxieties at first, at the end perfect triumph.

"We'll have a stroll out in the corridor," commands Bulpert. "That last piece has made me feel somewhat décolleté."

They gain the outer circle when Gertie has persuaded him to give to her the task of leading through the crowd; her smile obtains a free way that his truculent methods fail to obtain.

"I'm going to give up the Post Office," he announces impressively, "and I'm going in for the stage."

"If you can make money at it, there's no reason why you shouldn't."

Bulpert shows disappointment at the form of this agreement.

"I've come to the conclusion," he goes on, "that I'm not acting fairly towards the world in concentrating my abilities on the serving out of stamps and the issuing of postal orders. Besides which, I get no time for study. Evening before last, at the Finsbury Town Hall, I came as near to finding my memory fail as ever I've been. I'm burning the candle at both ends."

"Hope you'll have good luck."

"I shall deserve to have it," he concedes. "I sometimes stand at the side of the platform, and I see other parties trying in the same line, and I have to admit to myself that I do put something into my renditions of our poets and humorists that they fail to convey. Furthermore—"

"I don't want to miss the Henry the Eighth dances."

"Mention of him leads up to what I want to see you about. If I go on the stage—and to tell you the truth, I haven't completely made up my mind as yet—I shall want a certain amount of comfort at home. A professional man can't be bothered about domestic affairs. He has to keep his mind on his work."

"Where does Henry the Eighth come in?"

Bulpert takes her arm. "I had an idea of asking you, Gertie, to marry me."

A pause of nearly half a minute.

"Do you mind if I think it over before giving a definite answer?"

"I'm agreeable to that," he says, "providing you don't take too thundering long about it."

Thus, a new perplexity was added to those that Gertie Higham already bore upon her shoulders. There existed arguments in favour of accepting Bulpert's offer. He belonged to her own set; he was not in a position to comment upon her manner of speech, and there would be the satisfaction of knowing that she was in all respects his equal; in many his superior. Bulpert was perhaps a trifle pompous, more than a trifle conceited, but he was steady. If she married him, it would be a distinct score to arrange that it occurred ere Henry Douglass and Miss Loriner became united; were Gertie to send a small white box containing sugared cake after, the newspapers announced this fashionable wedding, the effect of the gift would be marred.

"I want to serve him out," she argued to herself, "for the way he treated me. It's only fair!"

Mrs. Mills was obviously delighted by the visits of Bulpert, and her ingenuity in leaving the young people together in the shop parlour proved that she was a mistress in the art of strategy. Bulpert excused himself to Gertie for omitting to invite her to the play, or for other outings, on the grounds that he was saving money; but he sometimes took her along to Paddington Station to see the night expresses start, and twice they went together to a large open place of entertainment in Edgware Road where you could, by dropping a penny in the slot, inspect a series of pictures that proved less exciting than the exhibited title; at the same expense you heard Miss Milly Manton's latest song, and George Limpsey's celebrated triumph in, "I wish I didn't talk so much to Clara!" On the evening of a day when Gertie had called upon the last firm of the list, she told Bulpert, as they met near Marble Arch, that if he cared to ask her now to be his wife she would accept him.

"Right you are," he said. "Then we'll consider the matter as practically settled."

They found Mr. Trew outside the shop when they returned; seeing them, he assumed the attitude of a figure taking snuff, and Gertie knew from this he was in good spirits. Mrs. Mills made the announcement that supper was waiting—a special meal because royalty had gone by that day to take train for Windsor—and Mr. Trew suggested Bulpert should have first cut at the food, the while he and the little missy strolled up and down to enjoy the evening air.

"I was bound to come along and see you," he said. "When I got the news I nearly fell off my seat. Should have done, only that I was strapped in. You remember Miss—what-was-her-name—we met at the Zoo that Sunday afternoon."

"Miss Loriner."

Mr. Trew stopped to make his announcement in a dramatic form.

"She's going to get spliced."

"So I guessed," remarked Gertie.

"But can you guess who to?"

"I think I can."

"Oh," he said regretfully. "Of course, if I'm not the first in the field with the news, there's an end of it. I sh'd say they'd be a very comfortable, 'appy, get-on-well-together couple, once they settle down."

She made a remark in a trembling voice.

"Of course you hope they will," he echoed heartily. "You and him have always got along well together. As I said, he hasn't took much time about it. Finished his book, he tells me."

"Mr. Trew, who are you talking about?"

"Why, your cousin Clarence, of course. I know it's correct because I got the information straight from the stable. And he would have called round to tell you, only he was busy. Said he wanted to see you soon, because he'd got a message. I won't be certain; there was a lot of traffic about, but I rather fancy it was something in the nature of a pressing invite."

CHAPTER VI

The days that followed were racing days for Gertie. At Great Titchfield Street a special order came in, and Madame held a kind of rehearsal, that the girls might know exactly what to do if the inspector called. The inspector represented the State, which, in the opinion of Madame and Miss Rabbit and all the assistants, male and female, was an interfering busybody hampering industry, and preventing honest workers from earning useful pay for unlimited overtime. To Great Titchfield Street, by day, came private letters by express messenger for Gertie, and more than one telegram; she generally found a communication awaiting her on the return home to Praed Street. Miss Rabbit accepted the statement that these came from Gertie's cousin, referring to nothing more romantic than a visit to the country; in private conversation with senior girls in the workroom, she said, rather bitterly, that Miss Higham surely took her for a born idiot.

Clarence proved himself alert and quick witted in retort, with an answer ready for every objection. When Gertie, as a final argument, put forward the matter of evening dress, he took her straightway to a celebrated firm (one-half of the lady passengers in public conveyances along the route gave, as their instruction and appeal to conductors, "Set me down as near as you can to Brown and Hodgkinson's!"), and there was purchased a blouse of white lace—costing so much that Gertie, on hearing the amount, had to clutch at one of the high chairs; and as Clarence paid readily with gold, the polite young woman on the other side of the counter assured him it was well worth the money. Gertie, at another establishment, bought a pair of slippers, saying to herself that they would come in handy, even though she did not go to Ewelme. Reluctance to accept the invitation conveyed through Clarence was supported at Praed Street by her aunt, who declared the girl would be like a fish out of water; that she would wish herself home again before she had been there the space of two minutes. But for Mrs. Mills's over-earnest counsel it is likely Gertie might have kept her threat (or promise) to back out at the last moment. On the Friday night, Mrs. Mills mentioned that the Douglass people were probably only asking Gertie in order to enjoy a laugh at her expense. The following morning, to her aunt's astonishment and open dismay, Gertie took a carefully-packed portmanteau along to the cloakroom at Paddington Station. In the afternoon she found herself, for the first time in her life, seated in a second-class carriage.

"Afraid you've had rather a rush," said her cousin.

"It isn't only that," she admitted, breathlessly. "I'm excited about this visit."

"Not more so than I am. All the same, I feel very much indebted to you, Gertie, for coming with me. The letter was worded in a way that meant I was to bring you, or not go at all. You see Mary—Miss Loriner—is only a companion at Morden Place. She couldn't have asked me on her own responsibility."

The girl closed her eyes and snuggled back in the corner. If Henry exhibited any special sign of affection, she would have to draw herself up to her full height and say, "Mr. Douglass, you're evidently not aware that you are speaking to an engaged lady." If he went so far as to propose marriage, the situation would be still more dramatic. "Mr. Douglass, you appear to have left it too late. I am already pledged to another!" There were alternative remarks prepared, and she felt certain that any one of them would be telling and effective. Clearly, he wanted to see her; otherwise so much trouble would not have been expended over the present visit; it was her business to make him see that a London girl was not to be taken up and dropped, and taken up again.

"Manners," she said resolutely, opening her eyes, and addressing a barge on the canal, "manners. That's what some people have got to be taught!"

The short train brought them slowly to the one platform of the station, and before she realized it, Henry Douglass was holding both of her hands, and looking down at her affectionately. He turned to give a welcome to her cousin, and Gertie told herself there was no necessity, for the present, to be dignified or reserved; that could come later. Outside the station, Miss Loriner was talking to a horse that seemed impatient to make its way in the direction of home; she and Clarence took seats at the back of the dogcart with a light rug spread over knees; they made no complaint of overcrowding.

"Can you really drive?" inquired Gertie with anxiety. "You never used to speak about it when Mr. Trew was talking."

"Life," answered Henry Douglass, "is too short to allow one to brag about everything. I do the best I can." They took the corner and went at a good pace through the town. "By Jove," he went on, enthusiastically, "you have no idea how I've missed you."

The first of the selected reproofs would have come in here appropriately, but a motor car was coming in the opposite direction with, as it seemed to her, the definite intention of running into their conveyance; she grabbed nervously at Henry's arm. When she looked again the car had gone, leaving dust as a slight memento of the encounter.

"Don't take it away!" he begged.

Here again either of the sentences might have been delivered; Gertie decided it would be sufficient to refrain from acceding to his request. Henry saluted with his whip folk who passed by, and told her who they were; stopped at one shop to take a parcel of wools intended for his mother. He had talked about Gertie to his mother, and she was anxious to meet Miss Higham.

"She'll be still more anxious to see me go away."

"You wouldn't say that," he asserted, "if you knew her."

"It's really Lady Douglass I'm afraid of. Look at that board, 'Trespassers will be prosecuted.' I feel it's meant for me."

"Trespassers," he said, "as a matter of fact, cannot be prosecuted. The board is all nonsense. Trespassers can only be prosecuted when they do some sort of damage."

She glanced around to watch a baby in the garden of a cottage; Clarence Mills and Miss Loriner were kissing. Gertie did not speak again until they reached the iron gates.

"I want to show you the tennis court," he said. "The man here can drive your cousin and Miss Loriner up to the house." She hesitated as he, stepping down, held out his hand. "My mother is waiting there!"

They found the grey-haired old lady resting on a low white enamelled seat, watching a game of singles between two stout men, who had the distressed look of those who play for the sake of health and figure. The ruddier of the two was pointed out as Mr. Jim Langham, brother to Lady Douglass; the other, a barrister with leanings in the direction of political work, and a present desire to be amiable towards everybody in the neighbourhood who possessed a vote.

"Now, you are to sit down here, Miss Higham," said the old lady, "and talk to me. I may interrupt you, now and again, but you mustn't mind that. One of the few privileges of age."

"I don't know what to talk about."

"Talk about yourself. I've heard about you from Henry, but I want to verify the information. You work for your living, don't you? Well now, that is interesting. I did the same before I was married. I married rather well, and then, of course, there was no necessity for me to go on with it."

"When my dear mother says she wants you to talk to her," explained Henry, "what she really means is that she wishes to talk to you. If you don't mind, I'll go over and teach these men how to play tennis."

Jim Langham came across directly that the game was finished, interrupting the two as they were getting on good terms with each other; on the way, he shouted an order to a gardener working near. He was effusive over the introduction to Gertie, showing his perfect teeth, and expressing the hope that she would not have to leave on Monday. The gardener brought a tumbler on a tray, and a syphon.

"At this time of the day?" said Mrs. Douglass, glancing at the contents of the glass.

"Good whisky," retorted Jim Langham, taking a small quantity of soda, "makes one feel like another man altogether."

"In that case," said the old lady, "by all means have the drink. My dear," to Gertie, "give me my stick and we'll walk up to the house and have tea."

"I'll come with you," remarked Jim Langham.

"You will stay where you are," ordered Mrs. Douglass.

Gertie, at Great Titchfield Street, had invented a house, doubled it, and multiplied it by ten; it came as a surprise to her to find that the residence was a solid building of fair extent with a parapet wall of stone in front, broad steps leading to the open doors. On the lawn tea was being set out by a man-servant; he lighted the wick underneath a silver kettle. Lady Douglass, in black, made an effective entrance down the steps in the company of a dog that looked like a rat.

"How perfectly charming of you to come and see us," she cried, extending a limp hand. "We do so want some one to brighten us up. Darling," to old Mrs. Douglass, "why didn't you tell them to send the bath-chair for you?"

"Myra," retorted the other, "I walk ten times as much as you do."

"Pray take care of yourself, for my sake."

"I hope to find some better incentive than that," said the old lady.

Lady Douglass approached the task of pouring out tea with the hopeless air of one who scarcely hoped to escape error, and when she had asked for and obtained particulars concerning tastes, Clarence Mills came, and his presence seemed to upset all the table plans; Mrs. Douglass arrested her action as she started to pour tea into the sugar basin. The arrival of Miss Loriner enabled her to resign the position. Going across to sit beside Gertie, she gave a highly interesting account of the way in which she had by sheer force of will conquered the cigarette habit; at present she consumed but twenty a day, unless, of course, special circumstances provided an excuse.

"Not for me, thanks," said Gertie, shaking her head. "I can't smoke; and if I could, I shouldn't."

"Tell me!" begged Lady Douglass; "how is that eccentric old gentleman we met at the Zoological Gardens?—Crew, or Brew, or some astonishing name of the kind?"

"I don't suppose," answered the girl defensively, "that you really want to know how he is, but Mr. Trew is quite well, and he isn't in the least eccentric, and he doesn't profess to be a gentleman."

Henry touched her shoulder with a gesture of appeal; she gave an impatient movement.

"But how extremely interesting," cried Lady Douglass, with something like rapture. "And do most of your friends work for a living?"

"All of 'em. I don't care for loafers."

"I myself have been up to my eyebrows in industry this week," said the other, self-commiseratingly. "I sometimes wish charity could be abolished altogether. It does entail such an enormous amount of hard labour. One might as well be in Wormwood Scrubbs."

She paused and looked at the girl intently.

"By the bye, where is Wormwood Scrubbs? One often hears of it."

"Over beyond Shepherd's Bush."

"Have you ever been there?"

"No," answered Gertie; "and I've never been to Portland, and I'm not acquainted with Dartmoor, and I don't know much about Newgate. Why do you ask?"

"I am hugely interested in prison life," declared the other.

"You mustn't be surprised," interposed Henry, addressing Gertie, "at any new subject that my sister-in-law mentions. I haven't heard her speak of this before; and it's only fair to her to say that when she takes up anything fresh, she drops it long before it has the chance of becoming stale. Another cup?"

He went to the table.

"A strange lad," said Lady Douglass musingly. "His heart is in the right place, but sometimes I wonder whether it is the right kind of heart. Do you mind dining at seven for once in your life. Miss Higham? It's a ridiculous hour, I know, but we must be at the hall sharp by eight. Miss Loriner will show you your room when you are ready. I have a thousand and one things to do," she added exhaustedly.

When Jim Langham joined the party and sat on the grass beside Miss Higham's chair, the girl rose, and Miss Loriner conducted her into the house; Henry regarded them with a cheerful smile as they left. The doors gave entrance to a square hall, with a broad staircase going up and turning suddenly to an open corridor that went around three sides. Gertie looked about her astonishedly.

"I've never been in a house like this before," she explained.

They went up the highly-polished staircase, Gertie holding at the banisters for safety.

"So Mr. Henry explained to me; and because he was so very good as to ask your cousin Clarence down, we have made a bargain between each other. I am to look after you, if you don't mind, and see that you get through all right."

"In a general way," confessed Gertie Higham, "I can look after myself, but just now it's likely I may be glad of a wrinkle or two." The other nodded.

"I have some on my forehead to spare, thanks to Lady Douglass. This is your room"—throwing open a door—"and mine is here, next door. Come along in, and let us have a talk."

Miss Loriner had a good deal to say, mainly in describing her present happiness. Clarence was a dear; Clarence was a clever dear, Clarence had brought a joy into her life that had previously been absent. Hitherto Miss Loriner, living in houses as a companion to some testy and difficult woman, found herself only annoyed by the attentions of men of the Jim Langham type; it was new and enchanting to be approached courteously. Gertie, when the other stopped to regain breath, managed to ask how Henry Douglass filled his time, and was surprised, and partially hurt, to discover that he still went up to Old Quebec Street on five days of the week.

"He might have called at the shop," she argued.

Miss Loriner, for the defence, commended him for his industry. Henry would, later, have to face the alternative of either giving up his office in London, or relinquishing duties in the country, but at present he was engaged in a double task; and if Gertie appreciated how difficult it proved to deal with Lady Douglass, she would not utter a word of blame in regard to Henry. One of Lady Douglass's inconvenient tricks was to shift responsibility. As a case in point, take the entertainment to which they were going that evening. Lady Douglass, having promised to organize it, had done not a single thing in the way of—

"Is the place on fire?" asked Gertie, startled.

"That's the first warning for dinner. You have twenty minutes to dress. Be sure to let me know if there is anything you want."

Gertie left, to return immediately with a concerned expression and the announcement that her portmanteau had been robbed of every blessed thing it contained. Miss Loriner accompanied her to make investigations, and, switching on the electric light, pointed out that the maid had unpacked the bag—the articles were on the dressing-table, and hanging up in the wardrobe. Gertie had only to ring, and the maid would come at once to help her to dress. Gertie said she had done this without assistance since the age of three.

Apologies were made later for the brevity of the evening meal, but it seemed to her a dinner that could only be eaten by folk who had starved for weeks. Her cousin sat opposite, and she watched his methods as each course arrived; envied the composure with which Clarence dealt with such trying dishes as vol au vent and artichokes. Her serviette was of a larkish disposition, declining to remain on her lap, and distress increased each time that Henry recovered it; generally, at these moments of confusion, Lady Douglass took the opportunity to send down some perplexing inquiry, and the girl felt grateful to Henry for replying on her behalf. Henry, it appeared, was to contribute to the programme at the hall, but he declined to give particulars; the disaster would, he said, be serious enough when it came. Jim Langham excused himself after dinner from joining the party on the grounds that he had to play billiards with the groom; and this reminded him of one of the groom's stories which (taking her aside) he thought Miss Higham as a Londoner would relish. The anecdote was but half told when Miss Higham turned abruptly.

"That's the right way," said old Mrs. Douglass to her approvingly.

At the door of the town hall carriages and motor cars were setting folk down, and Gertie, who had hoped the new blouse would enable her to smile at country costumes, felt depressed by their magnificence. In the front row Lady Douglass stood up, nodded, gave brief ingratiating smiles, and told people how remarkably well they were looking. Gertie, comforted by the near presence of her cousin, glanced over her shoulder, and wished she were with the shilling folk.

"Care to see the programme, Gertie?"

"I'll do the same as I do at a music hall," she said, "and take it as it comes. How did you think I managed at dinner, Clarence?"

"Capitally!"

"I had a knife and two forks left at the end," she said regretfully.

"A recitation," Clarence read from his programme. "Our friend ought to be here."

"Who do you mean?"

"Bulpert. You remember Bulpert, don't you?"

"I'd nearly forgotten him," she admitted.

There was an interval after men had sung and ladies had played, and a nervous youth had given imitations of popular actors who, it seemed, possessed the same tone of voice, and practised identical gestures. The curtain went up on an outdoor scene. A lady was reclining in a hammock.

"Why, it's Miss Loriner," whispered Gertie.

A man in tweeds came on backwards and collided with the hammock.

"Who's this supposed to be, Clarence?"

"Young Douglass. Made up with a beard."

An apology was made for the accident, and with the rapidity that the drama exacts in matters of the heart, the bearded gentleman was in less than fifteen minutes deeply in love with the lady of the hammock. "And if I promise to worship you all my life, will you then give me my heart's desire?" The lady, with a dexterous movement, came out of her resting-place. "You must first make a name in the world, and, hand upon heart, show yourself worthy of a woman's love!"

"What's the matter, Gertie?" asked Clarence Mills.

"I've made a—made a fearful muddle of nearly everything."

"Buck up!" urged Clarence. "Don't let people see you giving way."

The bearded man was leaving when the lady bethought herself to inquire his name; he proved to be none other than Mr. Francis Mainright, the well-known African explorer; and after a few more words the curtain came down on an affianced couple, with applause from all parts of the hall.

"Easy enough," said Gertie, in ceasing to clap hands, "for troubles to be put right on the stage. It's a bit harder in real life."

Lady Douglass accepted congratulations upon the success of her entertainment, and turned at the end, before leaving the hall, to request Gertie's attention for a moment. She was extremely anxious that her dear young brother-in-law should not commit an error that might last a lifetime. Apparently there was some one up in town who had managed to engage his affections: Lady Douglass did not know her; Miss Higham, of course, had not her acquaintance. The young woman, she believed, occupied an inferior position in life, and Lady Douglass would dearly like to have the opportunity of pointing out that supposing the two married, all the stories of ill-bred wives would be fastened upon Mrs. Henry Douglass. Every night, in every billiard-room, in every smoking-room in Berkshire, amusing stories, not always true, would be told of her mistakes; dull folk might find themselves reckoned as humorists by inventing anecdotes about her, and the general gaiety would find itself increased. Furthermore, there was this to be said. Supposing—

"Are you ready, dear girl?" asked Henry. He came down the steps from the platform, addressing his inquiry to Gertie.

"Quite!" answered Lady Douglass. "We were just chatting about your performance. Miss Higham seems to think you should have had more rehearsals. Doesn't exactly say so, but that is evidently what she means."

CHAPTER VII

There came a pleasant luxury in waking in a large room, with a maid pulling up the blinds, and reporting that the day promised to be grand. The maid could be looked upon as a friend, in that she knew the best and the worst concerning Miss Higham's clothes, and inquiries were put to her concerning breakfast; the answer came that this meal was ready at half-past eight; you went down at any time you pleased between this and ten o'clock. Mr. Henry breakfasted early; her ladyship and Mr. Langham were always the last. A start had to be made for church at twenty past ten. The maid asked whether Miss Higham would like the bathroom now, and Miss Higham, not quite certain whether it was good form to say "Yes" or "No," replied in the affirmative. As they went along the corridor, Gertie heard Henry Douglass singing in the hall below. The most astonishing detail in this wonderful house proved to be the size of the sponge.

She determined to hurry over her dressing and get downstairs quickly in order to talk privately with him, and consequent on this resolve, found herself, later, knocking at Miss Loriner's room and inquiring whether that young woman was ready to accompany her. After all, there would be time to make the announcement during the day.

"Have you slept well?"

"Like a top," declared Gertie. "For all the world as though I'd nothing on my mind."

"I don't suppose you have many serious murders to brood about."

"Not exactly murders," she replied. "Plenty of blunders."

Henry rose from the table as she entered; he dropped his open arms on seeing that she was not alone. Miss Loriner poured out coffee, and Henry, at the sideboard, recited the dishes that were being kept warm there. "Sausages," decided Gertie, "because it's Sunday morning!" She smiled, out of sheer content at being thus waited upon, and gave them a description of Praed Street, where the meal was continually interrupted by purchasers of journals, buyers of half-ounces of shag. She remarked that it would have been possible here to take breakfast out of doors, and Henry rang and gave instructions to Rutley, the butler, and the next moment, as it seemed, they were at table on the lawn, with sparrows pecking at stray crumbs. Henry, asking permission to smoke, lighted a pipe.

"I've only seen you with cigarettes before," she remarked. "Doesn't the tobacco smell good in the morning air! Do you know what I miss most of all? Sound of cabs going along to Paddington Station. I shouldn't care for the country, you know, not for always." She rattled on, jumping, as was her custom when happy, from one subject to another.

"It's miraculous to hear you talking again," he declared. "Last night we could scarcely get a word out of you."

"Tell me if I babble too much."

"You dear little woman!" he cried protestingly.

Clarence Mills came down, and Miss Loriner was relieved of the difficult task of keeping her eyes averted. Clarence, on the plea that he had some writing to do, wondered whether he might be excused from church, and Henry recommended the billiard-room as a quiet place for work; there was a writing-table at the end, and no one would interfere. Miss Loriner, when Clarence had finished his meal, offered to conduct him to the apartment; it was, it seemed, over the stables at the back of the house, and not easy for a stranger to find; moreover, Miss Loriner felt anxious to see how writing people started their work. Thus Henry Douglass and Gertie Higham would have been left alone, but that Jim Langham, exercising his gift of interference, appeared, rather puffed about the eyes, and one or two indications hinting that the task of shaving had not been without accident. Jim Langham's temper in the early hours seemed to be imperfect; he made only a pretence of eating, crumbling toast and chipping the top of an egg; he admitted he never felt thoroughly in form until after lunch. When Henry suggested that Gertie would like to see the grounds, Jim Langham followed them, pointing out the rose walk, and the summer-house (that was like a large beehive) with an air of proprietorship which Henry did not assume. Henry made an inquiry.

"I'm really chapel, if I'm anything," she answered; "but I shall like to go. Especially if you're to be there. It'll be the first time we've ever been in a place of worship together."

"We shall go together again," he said, "some day." She shook her head quickly.

Lady Douglass had breakfasted in her room, and came when they were ready and waiting; she complained severely that she seemed to be always the first when any expedition was in train. They walked around the carriage drive and across fields; at the porch, Lady Douglass offered to Gertie the hospitable inquiry in regard to the night's rest that Miss Loriner had made, and went on without waiting for a reply.

Gertie found herself wishing the service would continue for ever. It was soothing, beautiful, appropriate. "Forgiving us those things whereof our conscience is afraid, and giving us those good things which we are not worthy to ask," said the first collect of the day. "Grant that this day we fall into no sin, neither run into any kind of danger," said the third collect. "Fulfil now," said the prayer, "the desires and petitions of Thy servants, as may be most expedient for them." Announced the nervous young curate from the pulpit, "The eighth chapter of John, the thirty-second verse. 'The truth shall make you free.'" The curate had an artificial voice, and he glanced anxiously at Lady Douglass's aspect of jaded resignation; but it soon became evident he had something to say; Gertie, listening attentively, wondered whether he might, in some remarkable manner, have become acquainted with the particulars of her own case. Truth, he contended, was indispensable to the wise and comfortable conduct of life. Truth could only run on the main line; any deviation led to serious disaster. Truth might, at times, hurt others at the moment, but, in the end, it did nothing but good. Gertie felt impressed, and the effect of the address upon her was not decreased when, outside the church, and in accepting Lady Douglass's invitation to lunch, the young curate mentioned that he well remembered the great pleasure of meeting Miss Higham at a garden party, given up in town by the Bishop of London.

Folk had been asked for three o'clock to play tennis, and in walking across the lawn to look for them, Henry found the first opportunity of speaking to her alone.

"Tell me, dear girl," he said urgently, "why did you take no notice of my letters?"

"I never received any."

"Are you sure? I don't mean that," he went on hurriedly. "Only, I wrote to you three times, and no answer came."

"They must have been wrongly addressed. What number did you put on the envelopes?"

"But I also called, and saw your aunt."

"I didn't know that," admitted Gertie.

"Looks as though she stopped your notes. I'm sorry if that's the case."

"It worried me frightfully at the time," he said; "but it doesn't matter now."

"I rather fancy it does matter now." The tennis players came in sight, waving a salutation with their rackets.

Henry's mother apologized for a late appearance; no longer young, no longer indeed middle-aged, she found it necessary to save up strength, to use it economically. Gertie listened, content to be free from the presence of Lady Douglass, and genuinely interested in the other's conversation. Mark, the eldest son, she explained, arrived within a year after her marriage; then came two baby girls who went back to Heaven; then, after a long interval—

"It was because I had given away the rocking-horse," she declared.

—Then Henry. Mark was a good lad, but Henry had always been a dear lad. Poor Mark made the one great mistake of his life when he selected a wife, and Mrs. Douglass hoped the girl would understand why she felt anxious that Henry should not commit a similar error.

"I don't care whom he marries," declared the old lady resolutely, "providing he loves her, that she loves him, and that she is a good girl."

"That sort ought not to be hard to find."

"They are less plentiful," said the other, "than some people imagine. Now I want you to tell me something, my dear."

The girl was preparing to use caution when Jim Langham strolled up; his expectations of increased cheerfulness appeared to be realized, and his manner was almost rollicking. He suggested that Gertie should walk around with him; and the girl, to evade the threatened cross-examination, nodded an acceptance.

"You don't go in for many games, I suppose?"

"Wish I did," replied Gertie. "I shouldn't feel quite so much out of it."

"Henry will expect you to play him at billiards this evening. If you care to come across now," he offered, "I shall be delighted to give you some idea how to start."

As they turned to go along the path that led to the back of the house, Gertie glanced over her shoulder. Henry, watching their departure, missed an easy serve, and endured the reproaches of his partner.

"Rutley, I want the key of the billiard-room. Rutley, get it at once."

"I think I know where it was put last," said the butler.

They went up the steps, and waited until Rutley came. Jim Langham called him a slow-coach, a tortoise, a stick-in-the-mud, and a few other names. Rutley, unmoved, inquired whether his services were wanted as marker. Mr. Langham retorted that the butler might take it that whenever his help was required, definite instructions would be given.

The long room being well lighted by windows on both sides, the assistance of green shaded lamps that hung dependent above the table was not required. At the end, a raised platform with table and corner couches; on the mantelpiece rested a box of cigars, a silver case containing cigarettes and matches. A dozen cues stood upright in a military position on a stand. Jim Langham placed the red ball in its position, and Gertie took spot white. In showing her how to hold the cue, he touched her hand, and looked quickly to see if she resented this.

"You are going to make a very fine player," he declared presently. "All you need is practice."

Because of the pronounced scent of spirits, she drew away when he came too near; Jim Langham instantly became more deferential. By the luck that often comes to beginners, Gertie presently made five, potting the red and effecting a cannon; she beamed with the delight of success. Spot white was left in the centre of the table, and Langham, obtaining the long rest, explained the manner of using it. In doing so, he placed his hand upon her neck; the next moment he was on his knees conducting an active search under the table. Gertie, flushed with annoyance, went towards the door. Before she reached it, a knock came; the door was rattled impatiently.

"Open it from your side," ordered the high-pitched voice of Lady Douglass.

"The key is not here," answered Gertie.

"It must be there. Why is the door locked?"

"How should I know?" retorted the girl sharply. "You don't suppose I locked it, do you?" She heard Lady Douglass call for the useful Rutley; and when the butler came, there was a consultation outside. The door creaked, the lock gave way; Rutley, falling in with the door, just escaped collision with the perturbed girl. He was told to go.

"What does this mean?" demanded Lady Douglass. "Why are you in the billiard-room alone, Miss Higham?"

"I'm not alone. Your brother is here."

"That scarcely improves the look of affairs.—Jim, where are you?"

The gentleman, half emerging, made a mumbled, indistinct request for matches. Gertie, walking to the end of the room, found a box.

"There's your set of teeth," she pointed out, "just by the corner leg. It half frightened me when I saw I'd knocked the whole lot out."

"This is a serious matter," said Lady Douglass judicially. "The great thing will be to keep it from the knowledge of Henry."

"I'm not ashamed of my part in it!" She turned indignantly upon the red-faced man; his mouth was again furnished with the productions of the dentist, but he scowled in an alarming way. "What did you mean by it? Was this a dodge of yours, or of hers?"

"I simply, and by the merest chance," he complained to his sister, "happened to touch her near the shoulder, and you saw for yourself how she treated me. I shall go off and get a drink, and leave you both to clear it up as best you can. Serves her right!" He repeated this remark several times, with additions, as he stamped out of the room.

"My brother," said Lady Douglass, "is peculiar in his manners."

"I haven't met his sort before."

"But I wonder you did not know better than to trust yourself with him. Fortunately, you can rely upon me to say nothing about the affair. It would have been very unlucky if someone else had happened to come to the door."

"I don't particularly like being under any sort of obligation to you."

"We won't say anything more about it," ordered the other. "I have an enormous objection to a scandal."

"You're not alone in that respect," she retorted.

"And we will of course avoid all references to Wormwood Scrubbs."

"I don't know what you mean by that!"

The tennis folk, after they had replayed their games over the tea-table, left; Gertie was quiet, and her cousin inquired anxiously whether anything had occurred. Clarence urged her to keep up courage, declaring she had managed admirably up to the present.

"I feel as though there's thunder in the air," she said.

"There isn't," he assured her; "not a trace of it. It's a beautiful day. And," with enthusiasm, "Mary tells me she doesn't mind waiting until I make three hundred a year."

"Lucky boy!" she remarked absently.

They were still out on the lawn, and Henry had made a suggestion that they should all play golf-croquet when Rutley came to clear the table. Lady Douglass gave an instruction aside. "Very well, my lady," said Rutley; "it shall be seen to first thing in the morning. If we could only find the key I'd manage it myself." Henry asked whether anything was missing; his sister-in-law replied that it was nothing of importance— nothing that he need trouble about. Henry had quite enough to occupy his mind, and he must please allow her to take charge of some of the domestic anxieties.

"Rather unusual," said old Mrs. Douglass, "to find you so considerate."

"I get very little credit," sighed Lady Douglass.

As they waited on the croquet lawn to take their turn, Henry remarked to Gertie that no opportunity had yet been found for their long talk; looking down at her affectionately, he added that perhaps she could guess all that was in his mind. It had been perfectly splendid, he went on in his boyish way, simply magnificent, to be near to her for so long a period of time; they would have many week-ends similar to this. His mother had spoken approvingly of Gertie, and nothing else mattered. The girl kept her eyes on her mallet; she could not bring herself to the point of arresting his speech.

"We are waiting for yellow," said Lady Douglass resignedly.

Miss Loriner and Clarence seemed to lose interest in the game as it proceeded; later, they were missing when their colours were called. Lady Douglass, throwing down her mallet, delivered a brief oration. If people intended to play golf-croquet, they should play golf-croquet; if, on the other hand, they did not propose to play golf-croquet, they should say, frankly and openly, that they did not propose to play golf-croquet. Deploring the lack of candour and straight-forwardness, she pronounced the game at an end.

"Where are you going, Henry?" He answered promptly. "Come back! I don't want you to go to the billiard-room. You dare not ask me why; you must just comply with this one wish of mine."

"Have you any reasons?"

"The best of reasons." She exhibited a considerable amount of agitation; her head went from side to side. "Do please obey me. If you do not, you will regret it to the last hour of your life."

He stared at her curiously.

"I rather fancy," interposed Gertie, breaking the pause, "that I'm the best one to explain." She was standing beside old Mrs. Douglass, and as she spoke she gripped at the back of the wicker chair. "I don't like this mystery where I am concerned. Lady Douglass came to the door of the billiard-room whilst Mr. Langham and me—Mr. Langham and I were there. The door was locked. She had it burst open."

Henry held out his hand appealingly. "That can't be all," he urged.

"It's all that matters."

"Where is Jim?" he demanded of Lady Douglass.

"I am not my brother's keeper, but I believe he has gone down into the village."

"There's something more I've got to say," Gertie went on. Her voice trembled; she made an effort to control it. "It's kind of you to ask me down here, but I wish you had invited Clarence alone. He knows how to behave in company like this; I don't. I'm not in it. It was foolish of me to come. It's like anybody trying to go Nap without a single picture card in their hand. And I want to tell you something more—I'm engaged! Engaged to a youngish man in my own station of life."

"No, no!" he cried.

"My dear," said old Mrs. Douglass, looking up concernedly, "surely you're not in earnest!"

"I think," remarked Lady Douglass impartially, "that she is acting with great wisdom."

"I was wishing to-day," the girl went on, raising her voice, "that I hadn't got myself engaged. It happened because of a misunderstanding, and I did it on the impulse of the moment; all the same, it can't be helped. And I was pretty jolly before I met Henry, and—I don't know—I may be pretty jolly again. If I go right out of his life now—why, I shall only think, I shall only remember—"

Old Mrs. Douglass turned in her chair and patted the girl's hand.

"I shall only remember how happy I was all the time after I was lucky enough to meet him. It's over and done with now, and I'm going back home, where I can be trusted. I must be trusted. Here, you don't quite believe me." She bent down to old Mrs. Douglass. "Not even you. I'm a foreigner at this place; a foreigner, trying to learn your habits and customs, and trying to forget my own. Perhaps, one day, you'll see that although I wasn't very refined, and not too well brought up," she raised her face, and her chin went out, "all the same, I did know how to keep myself straight."

Young Mills came across the croquet lawn.

"Want you for a moment, Clarence," she said.

Henry Douglass, descending the staircase slowly and thoughtfully at eight o'clock, asked Rutley whether Miss Higham was in the drawing-room. Rutley answered that the young lady and Mr. Mills had gone. Walked to Cholsey to catch the evening train to town. One of the under-gardeners carried their luggage.

"Quite thought you knew, sir," mentioned Rutley.

CHAPTER VIII

Frederick Bulpert, having obtained two professional engagements at seven shillings and sixpence each, resigned his situation in the Post Office, and this left him free to call at Praed Street whenever he cared to do so. Mrs. Mills described him as a hearty eater, but she made much of him, apparently out of gratitude. Gertie had spoken to her about Henry's letters—

"She looked rather white," said Mrs. Mills to Mr. Trew confidentially; "but I must admit she kept her temper wonderfully well, considering!"

—And the girl took charge of the intercepted envelopes with their contents. Her aunt declared, with emphasis, that all along she had acted for the best. Gertie remarked that people said this whenever they had done their worst: this was the only reproach given, and Mr. Trew, as a candid friend, assured Mrs. Mills she had been let off very lightly. Mr. Trew had anxieties of his own. The new motor omnibuses still broke down occasionally, and he was able, in passing, to make offers for the conveyances at an extremely low figure; but many of them ran without accident, and ran speedily, and he was losing customers hitherto considered faithful and regular. Summing up, he came to the conclusion that the world was becoming a jolly sight too clever; the only comfort he found was that it could not possibly exist much longer. Regaining cheerfulness, he mentioned that if Mrs. Mills happened to hear of an American heiress who wanted a good-looking English husband with a special and particular knowledge of horses, well acquainted with London, and fond of the sea, why, it would be kind of her to drop him a postcard, giving the name and address.

"When you've finished talking nonsense," she said, "perhaps you'll kindly tell me how I'm to manage in order to get these two young people married. She'll be happy enough, once she settles down; but, meanwhile, I don't like seeing her so quiet and thoughtful."

"I have never denied," he remarked, "that you are the prize packet of your sex, and in many respects you've got almost the intelligence of a man. But in a matter of this kind—remember, she's as pretty as they make 'em—you're a born muddler. Leave it to me, and I'll do the best I can for you."

Wherefore, Mr. Trew made appointments with Bulpert and held secret discussions with him, sheltering his words with a broad, big hand, enjoying greatly the sense of management, and, even more, the atmosphere of conspiracy. Bulpert, on his side, began to realize his importance, and treated Praed Street with a condescension that was meant to represent a correct and proper pride. One evening, seated at the counter there, and waiting for the return of Gertie, he gave a formal warning to the effect that any cigar presented to him was, in future, to be taken from the threepenny box.

At Great Titchfield Street, Gertie tried to divert her mind from personal anxieties by throwing energy into work, with more than common resolution. A large commission arrived from a ruler of an Eastern nation, who considered a new and elaborately ornamental sash would revive a feeling of loyalty in his army and patriotism in his country. The girls were not permitted except on strictly limited occasions to work after nine o'clock in the evening, and extra assistants had to be engaged; the men upstairs who made the leather foundations were watched and encouraged; Madame begged Gertie to recommend them to keep off the drink, adding that they would take more notice of this advice if it came from Miss Higham and not from Madame herself. All the looms were at their noisy spider work; reels of gold thread were ordered in twenties; the bobbins began to dance around the maypole, sewing-machines sang lustily; the telephone only ceased ringing to deliver messages. Miss Rabbit became hysterical, vehement, cross; Gertie's intervention became necessary to prevent a strike amongst the pinafored young women.

"We can be led, Miss Higham," they announced determinedly, "but we won't be drove. You tell her to keep a civil tongue in her head, and all will go well. We're not going to be treated as though we was Russians."

The rush of work had, for consequence, a distinct advantage to Gertie, apart from useful occupation of the mind. She stayed late to finish books which could not be entered up in the day, and this meant that, on returning home, the good news was frequently communicated that Mr. Bulpert had gone; there was also the comfortable fact that she felt sufficiently tired to go straight to bed. Bunny, at Great Titchfield Street, on the occasions when she herself had to depart and leave Madame and Miss Higham together, was a picture of woeful apprehension; if she managed to gain the private ear of the girl, she reminded her that no good ever yet came to one who failed to keep a solemn promise.

"Don't you worry," answered Gertie. "I'm not a parrot."

"I shan't feel happy about you," said the forewoman solicitously, "until I hear you've got another berth. The smash-up will come as a surprise to the others, but I don't care a snap of the fingers about them or about myself. It's you I'm thinking about!"

Madame one night, at the sloping desk, referred vaguely to a wish that, as she hastened to add, could never in any circumstances be gratified. Urged by Gertie, on the other side, to put the desire into words, Madame took off spectacles which she wore only when the rest of the staff had gone, and said wistfully that if she could but get a paragraph into the newspapers containing the name of the firm, she thought it would be possible to die happy. Having ascertained this did not mean that suicide would follow, Gertie sent a note to Clarence Mills, absent since the evening of the impulsive departure from Ewelme.

No answer came, and Gertie was assuming that her cousin intended, in this way, to prove he was not on terms of peace with her, when one of the loom workers brought in, after lunch hour, an evening journal, obtained by him because he required advice regarding the investment of small sums on the prospects of racehorses.

"Here's a bit about us, miss," he said exultantly, with thumb against the paragraph. "Here we are. Large as life, and twice as natural!"

The paragraph was found in other newspapers, and indeed it went about Great Britain later and found its way to the Colonies. "An Oriental Omen" it was headed, and Madame's only regret appeared to be that it could not be held to be distinguished by the quality of absolute truth. But there it stood in print, and there was the name of Hilbert and Co., the old established firm, making a speciality of manufacturing military accoutrements, dating from the glorious year of Waterloo, and Madame's delight proved beyond the powers of expression; her gratitude to Miss Higham was conveyed by a kiss. One competing firm, it was discovered, wrote a sarcastic letter to the papers that must have taken hours to compose, throwing doubts on the accuracy of the report and inquiring whether it was a fact that Wellington's achievement followed the Franco-Prussian War, and this might have been inserted but for the suggestion of self-advertisement made with something less than the dexterity that belonged to Clarence's pen.

"I tell you what, Miss Higham," said Madame definitely. "You must come to supper at my house the very next Sunday evening that ever is. Your aunt won't mind for once. I'll write down the address. My proper name is Jacks. Yes, dear, I'm married, to tell you the truth, only I don't want it talked about here."

Frederick Bulpert, when he arrived on the Sunday evening, entered a warm protest against what he described as this eternal gadding about. On ascertaining the destination, he admitted circumstances altered cases; where business was concerned, private interests had to give way. He explained that some of his present irritation was due to the fact that, at a Bohemian concert the previous evening, an elderly gentleman had been pointed out to him as the representative of an important Sunday newspaper; the comic singer who gave the information, encountered a few minutes since in Marylebone Road, confessed that it was one of his jokes. "And all the drinks I stood," complained Bulpert, "and all the amiable remarks I made, absolutely wasted!" Gertie, apparelled in her finest and best, went at the hour of seven, after Bulpert and her aunt had quarrelled regarding the best and speediest mode of transit, to make her way to King's Road, Chelsea. There, in a turning she twice walked by without noticing, she found a house with several brass knobs at the side of the door. A maid answered her ring.

"Sounds as though they're in the studio," remarked the maid, with a wink. "What name?"

The servant opened the door and gave the announcement, but in the tumult it was not heard. Madame's husband was informing Madame in a loud voice that the most unfortunate day in his life was the occasion when he allowed her to drag him into a registrar's office. Gertie went back a few steps, and the maid repeated the name.

"You dear!" cried Madame, coming forward pleasantly. "This is my husband. You know him by name, I expect." She whispered, "The celebrated river painter. Most successful. And such a worker. Never idle for a moment."

"How d'ye do?" said Mr. Jacks, coming forward casually. "Sorry I'm just going out. What's the night like?"

Madame switched on the electric light, and Gertie could see that the room suggested a large cucumber frame with a sloping glass roof and windows at the far end. On a raised square platform in a corner stood a draped lay figure, not, apparently, quite sober.

"Well," said Madame's husband, after glancing again at the visitor, "if it's fine, I don't know that there's any special necessity for me to go. What do you say, darling?" This to his wife.

"Please yourself, Digby, my sweet. If you think you can put up with our company, I am sure Miss Higham and myself will be delighted if you can stay. Mr. Jacks," she explained to Gertie, "is naturally attracted to his club, not only because he finds there all the latest news concerning his profession, but because it gives him an opportunity of coming into contact with other bright, vivacious spirits." She took Gertie's coat and hat. "Perhaps we can get him to tell us some of his best stories presently."

Her husband smoothed his hair at the mirror with both hands, and gave style and uniformity to the two halves of his moustache. This done, he turned and asked the girl whether she did not consider Whistler an overrated artist. Just because he happened to be dead, people raved about him. Would not allow any one else to produce impressions of the Thames round about Chelsea. Mr. Jacks said, rather bitterly, that when he too was no more, folk would doubtless be going mad about him, and Jubilee Place might become impassable owing to the crowd of dealers waiting their turn there.

"And what good do you imagine that will do to me?" he demanded. "Eh, what? No use you saying that I ought to be content with the praise of posterity."

"I didn't say so. How many hours do you work a day?"

"I can't work unless the fit takes me," argued Madame's husband weakly.

"Are you subject to them? Fits, I mean?"

Madame, assisting the maid in setting the table, took up the case for the defence, and pointed out to Miss Higham that one profession differed from another. In the case of painting, for instance, you could not expect to be ruled by office hours; you had to wait until inspiration came, and then the light was, perhaps, not exactly what you required. Besides, friends might drop in at that moment for a smoke and a chat.

"Sounds like an easy life," remarked Gertie.

"You forget the wear and tear of the brain," said Madame.

"But we get that in our business."

"Hush!" whispered the other. "He doesn't like hearing that referred to."

Conversation during the meal was restricted to the subject of the production of pictures and their subsequent disposal; Madame showed great deference to the arguments of her husband, occasionally interposing a mild suggestion which he had no difficulty in knocking down. At moments of excited contention Madame's husband became inarticulate, and had to fall back upon the gestures of the studio, that conveyed nothing to the visitor.

"How much do you make a year?" she asked, when an opportunity came. He paused in his task of opening another bottle of stout, and regarded her with something of surprise.

"My good girl," he replied, "I don't estimate my results by pounds, shillings, and pence."

"Do you earn a hundred in twelve months?"

"Wish I did," confessed Madame's husband. "In that case, I shouldn't have to be beholden to other people."

"How would you manage if you weren't married?"

He looked at the mantelpiece, and inquired of his wife if the clock was indicating the correct time. Receiving the answer, Madame's husband became alarmed, declaring it a fortunate thing that he had remembered a highly important appointment. It represented, he said, the chance of a lifetime, and to miss it would be nothing short of madness; he bade Miss Higham good evening in a curt way, and Madame accompanied him to the front door. There they had a spirited discussion. Madame considered an allowance of half a crown would be ample; he said, in going, that his wife was a mean, miserable cat.

"I'm afraid, my dear, you shunted him off," remarked Madame, coming back to the studio. "You don't seem to know how to manage men, do you?"

"Had my suspicions of that before now."

"Of course, they're very trying but"—helplessly—"I don't know. Sometimes I wish I'd kept single, and then again at other times, when I've had a hard day of it, I feel glad I'm not coming home to empty rooms. Taking the rough with the smooth, I suppose most women think that any husband is better than no husband at all."

"Rather than get hold of one who didn't earn his living," declared Gertie with vehemence, "I'd keep single all my life."

"He did nearly sell a picture," argued the other, "once!"

They took easy-chairs, and Madame found a box of chocolates. Mr. Jacks, it appeared, was not Madame's first love. Mr. Jacks's predecessor had been ordered out years ago to take part in a war that improved the receipts entered up in Hilbert's books; on the debit side, the loss of a good sweetheart had to be placed. Madame dried her eyes, and in less than half a minute the two were on the subject which absorbed their principal interests. Price of gold thread, difficulty with one of the home workers, questions of aiguillettes, sword belts, sashes, grenades; hopes that the King would shortly issue a new order concerning officers' uniforms. Madame said that, nowadays, profits were cut very close; she could remember, in her father's time, when, if there was not a balance at the end of the year of over a thousand pounds, serious anxiety ensued. Madame brought out a large album to show pictures of gorgeous apparel that belonged to days before thrift became a hobby.

"Seems to me," she said, without leading up to the remark, "that Miss Rabbit is the weak link in our chain." Gertie did not make any comment. "I'm going to tell you something. I want to give her other work to do, and get you to take her place. It will amount to an extra ten shillings a week, Miss Higham."

"Do you really mean it?"

"It's why I asked you to come here this evening. You see, you have improved so much this summer. Improved in style, speech, everything!"

"There's a reason for that!"

Gertie Higham walked up and down the studio with excitement in her eyes. She wanted to ask Madame how long the firm was likely to endure, but to do this might lead to the betrayal of confidence; meanwhile she fired inquiries, and Madame, eager to gain her approval of the suggestion, answered each one promptly. Bunny was not to be reduced in wages; only in position. One of the new duties would be to run about and see people; Madame's nerves were not quite all they used to be, and the hurried traffic of the street frightened her. Next to Madame, Gertie would be considered, so to speak, as head cook and bottle-washer. Gertie, collecting all this information, wondered how it would be possible to let Henry Douglass know that she was making important progress. Possibly it could be managed through Clarence Mills and Miss Loriner; she might meet him in London, at some unexpected moment.

"Do you object, Madame," she asked, "if I run off now, and tell aunt about it?"

"You accept the offer?"

"Like a shot!" answered Gertie.

"You dear!" cried Madame.

Frederick Bulpert was on the point of leaving when she reached Praed Street; he came back into the shop parlour to hear the news. Her aunt kissed her, and said Gertie was a good, clever girl; Bulpert declared the promotion well earned.

"This is distinctly frankincense and myrrh," he acknowledged. "I feel proud of you, and I don't care who hears me say so. Let me see; your birthday's next week, isn't it? How about arranging something in the nature of a conversazione, or what not?"

"I hope," said Mrs. Mills, escorting him through the shop, "that, later on, you'll do your best to make her happy."

"But it's her," protested Bulpert, "it's her that's got to make me happy."

CHAPTER IX

Clarence Mills, invited to be present at the birthday evening, wrote in frolicsome terms, from which the young hostess judged that with him the progress of love was satisfactory. "My dear young relation, near Paddington Station, of course I will come to your show. If forced to leave early, you won't think me surly; I have to meet some one you know!" To this Gertie sent a card begging Miss Loriner to include herself in the invitation, and that young woman forwarded a telegram from Ewelme with the word "Delighted."

"Now"—to herself hopefully—"now I shall hear some news about him!"

Gertie decided the evening should differ from evenings which had preceded it, in that the entire expense was to be borne by herself; and Mrs. Mills therefore only offered a feeble objection when the girl arranged that the front room upstairs was to be turned out, rout seats hired, and a few articles of furniture, including the piano-forte (which, at one perilous moment, threatened to remain for the rest of its life at the turn of the staircase), transferred from the shop parlour. Bulpert announced his intention of taking charge of the musical and dramatic part of the entertainment. Bulpert no longer considered himself a visitor at Praed Street, and on one occasion he entered a stern protest when he found Mr. Trew's hat there, resting upon the peg which he considered his own. Twice he had suggested that Gertie should lend him half a sovereign, reducing the amount, by stages, to eighteenpence; but she answered definitely that advances of this kind interfered with friendship, and she preferred not to start the practice.

"I could let you have it back in a fortnight."

"Perhaps!" she said. "And if you did, you would be under the impression that you were doing me a great favour."

"I like to see a girl economical," he remarked, frowning, "but there's a diff'rence between that and being miserly. And," with resolution, "I go further, and I say that if there's anybody who's got a just and fair and proper claim on your consideration, it is F. W. B."

"There's some one who comes before you."

"The name, please?"

"Myself," replied Gertie.

The question of conciliating Miss Rabbit at Great Titchfield Street had been solved, and matters there were going smoothly. Miss Rabbit continued to hold her title of forewoman, although she was no longer forewoman; and Miss Higham took the label of secretary, which well described duties she did not perform. The girls in the workroom made no concealment of their satisfaction with the change, and men at the looms upstairs came individually to Gertie and said, "Look here, miss! If ever you have any difficulty or awk'ardness or anything of the kind with the other chaps, just give the word, and I'll put it all right."

Bunny, for the preservation of friendship, went down on the birthday party list, and Miss Radford (who had not been seen for some time) and two girls (formerly at school with Gertie, and then known as a couple of terrors, but now grown tall and distinguished, and doing well in a notable shop in Westbourne

Grove), and, of course, Mr. Trew, and two friends of Bulpert's, whom he guaranteed capable of keeping any party on the go. Mrs. Mills checked the names, expressed satisfaction.

"I was half afraid," she said, "you'd want to send a note to that young gentleman who lives near where I was brought up."

"If he came here," replied the girl steadily, "I should only fall in love with him again, and that would complicate matters."

"I think you're wise," approved Mrs. Mills.

A charwoman from Sale Street came in to scrub floors, to see to fireplaces, and to renovate apartments generally—a slow worker, on account of some affection of the heart, but an uncommonly good talker. When human intercourse failed she addressed articles of furniture, asking them how much they cost originally, and, sarcastically, whether they were under the impression that they looked as good as new; to some she gave the assurance that if she were to meet them at a jumble sale, she would pass by without a second glance. The charwoman suggested, at the completion of her task, and rolling up her square mat with the care of one belonging to an Oriental sect, that her help should be engaged for the party; Mrs. Mills replied that if they required help, some one of more active methods and of less years would be approached.

"Right you are!" she said, taking her money from the counter. "In that case, I'll send along my Sarah."

To suit the young hostess, and to meet the convenience of one or two of the guests, the party began at an hour that was quite fashionably late. Miss Radford came early, excusing herself for this breach of decorum on the grounds that it made her painfully nervous to enter a room when strangers were present; apart from which, to arrive in good time meant that one had a chance of looking at oneself in the mirror. Did Gertie consider that her (Miss Radford's) complexion was showing signs of going off? A lady friend, who, from the description given, seemed to be neither a friend nor a lady, had mentioned that Miss Radford was beginning to look her full age; and remarks of this kind might be contradicted but could not be ignored.

"Don't you ever get anxious about your personal appearance?" she inquired.

"Not specially."

"I suppose," agreed Miss Radford, "that being properly engaged does make you a bit less anxious."

Clarence came with Miss Loriner, and the young hostess flushed at the young woman's first words. Henry sent his best regards. Henry, it appeared, no longer spent week-ends at Ewelme—this because of some want of agreement with Lady Douglass; and he was now busy in connection with a sanatorium at Walton-on-Naze, which demanded frequent journeys from Liverpool Street. Gertie, in taking Miss Loriner to get rid of hat and dust-cloak in the adjoining room, felt it good to find herself remembered. Miss Loriner wanted a small fan, and searching the hand-bag which she had brought, first looked puzzled, and then became enlightened.

"I've brought Lady Douglass's bag by mistake," she cried, self-reproachfully. "Here are her initials in the corner—'M. D.'; not 'M. L.'" Miss Loriner gave an ejaculation.

"What is it you've found there?"

"This," announced the other deliberately, "is the missing key of the billiard-room at Morden Place!"

The two girls looked at each other, and Gertie nodded.

"I've been blaming her brother all along for that trick."

"My dear girl," demanded Miss Loriner, "aren't you fearfully excited and indignant about it?"

"Doesn't seem to matter much now. But," smiling, "she is a character, isn't she? I pity you if she often does things like that."

"I shall be uncommonly glad," admitted the other, "when Clarence earns three hundred a year. Do you know that if you had stayed on at Morden Place, this key would most likely have been found in your portmanteau."

Frederick Bulpert, arriving with his friends, asserted his position by attempting to kiss Gertie; she drew back, and Bulpert said manfully that if she could do without it he could also afford to dispense with the ceremony. He introduced his companions as two of the very best and brightest, and they intimated, by a modest shrug of the shoulders, that this might be taken as a correct description. The sisters of Westbourne Grove came bearing a highly-ornamental cardboard case with a decoration of angels, and containing a pair of gloves. They mentioned that if the size was not correct the gloves could be changed, and at once took seats in the corner of the room, whence they surveyed the company with a critical air, sighing in unison, as though regretting deeply their mad impulsiveness in accepting the invitation. On this, other presents were offered; Bulpert said his memento would come later on. One of his friends sat on the music-stool, and Sarah, the charwoman's daughter, entering at the first chord with a tray that held sandwiches and cakes, said to him casually, "Hullo, George, you on in this scene?" and handed around the refreshments. Bulpert's friend, disturbed by the incident, waited until the girl left the room, and then explained that he had met her in pantomime, the previous Christmas, at the West London Theatre; he argued forcibly that people encountered behind the footlights had no right to claim acquaintance outside. "Otherwise," contended Bulpert's friend, "we're none of us safe." He was induced to give his song, and the first lines,—

"I went to Margate, once I did, to spend my holidee,
Such funny things you seem to see beside the silver sea"

suggested that he was not one disposed to worship originality or make a fetish of invention. Bulpert, at the end, pointed out that his friend had omitted the last verse; the man at the pianoforte said there were some places where he was in the habit of giving the last verse; this, he declared flatteringly, was not one of them. Gertie's aunt came upstairs to announce that, the occasion being special, she had taken it upon herself to put up the shutters. If they excused her for half a second this would give her sufficient space to tittivate and smarten up.

"Say when you want me to liven 'em up, Gertie," remarked Bulpert.

"Go and be nice to those two sisters in the corner."

"When we're married," he said, "we'll often give little affairs of this kind. I'm a great believer in hospitality myself."

As he did not appear to make a great deal of headway with the Westbourne Grove ladies, he was recalled and the task handed over to Clarence Mills. Clarence scored an immediate success. The sisters, it seemed, prided themselves upon being tremendous readers; Clarence was acquainted with some of the writers who, to them, were only names. And the young hostess would have been able to survey the room with contentment, but for the fact that Miss Radford suddenly became depressed—with hands clasped over a knee she rocked to and fro in her chair. Gertie discovered that to her friend had just come the terrifying thought that no one loved her, nobody cared for her, and for all practical purposes Miss Radford might as well be dead and buried, with daisies growing over her grave. Gertie argued against this melancholy attitude, and the other explained that it came to her only at moments when every one else was jolly and cheerful, adding defiantly that she could not avoid it, and did not mean to avoid it.

"People," declared Miss Radford with truculence, "have to take me as they happen to find me!"

Bulpert's second friend, advancing with a pack of cards, asked if Miss Radford would kindly select one and tell him the description. "The Queen of Hearts? Nothing," said Bulpert's second friend, with a gallant bow, "nothing could be more appropriate." Miss Radford cried, "Oh, what a cheeky thing to say!" and at once bade farewell to melancholy.

A wonderful man, the second friend—able to do everything with cards that ordinary folk deemed impossible. If you selected a card and tore it up; and he presently—talking all the while—produced a card, and said in the politest way, "I think that is yours, madam?" and you remarked that this was the four of clubs, whereas you selected the five, he exclaimed, with pretence of irritation, "Well, what is there to grumble at?" and, looking again, you saw that it had changed to the five of clubs. There was nothing to do but to applaud and wonder. He swallowed cards, and produced them with a slight click from his elbow, the middle of his back, and his ankle. He allowed Miss Loriner to find the four aces and put them at the bottom of the pack, and the next moment asked Mr. Trew, who had just arrived, to produce them from the inside pocket of his coat. Mr. Trew had some difficulty in finding them, but the conjurer assisted, and there were the four aces; and Mr. Trew, after denying the suggestion that he had come prepared to play whist, admitted the young man was a masterpiece. Mr. Trew's watch was next borrowed and wrapped in paper; the poker borrowed in order to smash it; the violent blow given. Miss Radford was asked to be so very kind as to assist by looking in the plate of nuts that stood on the table, and there the watch was discovered, safe and sound. Some thought-reading followed, not easy to understand because of the incessant monologue kept up by the gifted youth; but the results were satisfactory, and by pressing the folded pieces of paper very hard against his forehead, he was able to announce the names written within.

"This is yours, I think, Miss Higham. Now, I don't guarantee success, mind you, in every case, but—the name, I think, is Henry"—he contorted his features—"Henry Douglass. Is that right, may I ask?"

"Quite correct!" replied Gertie.

"What did you want to write his name for?" demanded Bulpert, seated next to her.

"It was the first that came into my head."

"Kindly keep it out of your head in future," he ordered, "or else there'll be ructions."

Did the ladies object to smoke? asked some one. The ladies answered, separately and collectively, that they adored smoke; the Westbourne Grove young women, now in excellent fettle, admitted that, at times, they themselves enjoyed a cigarette, but could not be persuaded to give a public exhibition of their powers. They did, however, agree to give a short sketch entitled "Who is Who?" and the hearthrug was given up to them; and if they had not made so many corrections—neither appeared to be well acquainted with her own part in the piece, but each was letter perfect in the part of the other—the duologue would have been a great success.

"And now," said Mrs. Mills, "let's see about refreshments. Mr. Trew, where's that corkscrew of yours?"

"Isn't it about time I was asked to do something?" demanded Bulpert, with an injured air.

"Let us see you do your celebrated trick," suggested Gertie's aunt, with irony, "of eating nearly everything there is on the table. That's what you're really clever at."

Miss Radford, by a sudden inspiration, suggested the ladies should wait upon the gentlemen, and herself took a plate to Bulpert's conjuring friend; the example was imitated. Mr. Trew, attended to by Gertie, declared it a real treat to see her looking like his own little friend once again.

"Makes me think," he said, "that if there wasn't quite so much diplomacy about on the part of those of us who reckon we know everything, you young uns would get a far better chance. Speaking as one who's been a fusser all my life, that's my candid opinion."

"If you interfered, Mr. Trew, you would interfere wisely."

He emptied his glass in one drink, and set it upon the mantelpiece. "I wouldn't kiss the book on that, if I was you," he replied. "But what you can be very well certain about is that if I saw the chance of doing anything for you—"

Miss Rabbit was announced by Sarah, and Gertie had to leave Mr. Trew in order to make much of her colleague. Bulpert, having edged other folk from the hearthrug, announced that he was about to give, with the aid of memory, a short incident of the American Civil War; to his astonishment and open indignation, one of the Westbourne Grove girls arrested him with the suggestion that instead they should all have a game. Challenged to indicate one, she asked what was the matter with musical chairs. So chairs were placed down the centre of the room, facing opposite ways alternately. Gertie went to the pianoforte, and all prepared to join, with the exception of Bulpert, who, in the corner, and his back to the others, ate sandwiches.

Admirable confusion, thanks to Gertie's ingenious playing. As they started to march warily in a line up and down the row, she, after giving the first bar, stopped, and they had to rush for seats. Clarence Mills was left out and a chair withdrawn. The next trial was much longer, and only when caution was being relaxed did the music cease; Miss Loriner, defeated at this bye-election, had to take a seat near to Clarence. The joyousness was so pronounced that Bulpert found himself to take some interest, and when Mrs. Mills, left in with Mr. Trew, eventually won the game, he urged it should be restarted, and that some other lady should play the music. On the first arrest by Miss Rabbit at the pianoforte, he sat himself on a chair already occupied by Gertie. At the moment, Sarah appeared again at the doorway.

"A young man," she announced importantly. "A gentleman this time."

Henry Douglass came in. Gertie struggled to disengage herself, but Bulpert declined to move.

"Mrs. Mills, I must apologize for calling at this late hour."

"Don't mention it, sir."

"I have just had a message from my sister-in-law, and I wanted to see Miss Loriner. Lady Douglass has been taken seriously ill."

Mr. Trew took Bulpert by the collar and sent him with a jerk against the wall. Gertie, flushed and confused, shook hands with Henry.

"I'm not going to break up your evening," he said, looking at her eagerly. "The matter is urgent, or I wouldn't have dared to call."

"We are always," she stammered, "always pleased to see you, Mr. Douglass."

"My dear mother asked me to give you her love when I met you. There is a car waiting," he went on, addressing Miss Loriner; "could you manage to come now? We can do it in little over a couple of hours."

Gertie took Miss Loriner into the adjoining room.

"If she's really ill," said the girl, "don't tell him anything about the key. He can hear it all, later on. And nobody at Praed Street knows anything about the affair."

Bulpert declined to escort Miss Rabbit to her omnibus, and, in spite of hints from Mrs. Mills, remained when all the other guests had departed. He took opportunity to criticize the management of the evening, and to deplore the fact that his services had not been utilized. Making an estimate of the total cost, he again referred to his suggestion in regard to a series of similar entertainments later on.

"If you find you can afford it," agreed Gertie.

"If I can afford it!" he echoed surprisedly. "There's no question of me affording it. Why don't you talk sense? You'll be earning the same good salary after we're spliced as you're earning at the present moment."

"No!" she answered definitely. "When I'm married I give up work at Great Titchfield Street."

"Why, of course," agreed Mrs. Mills. "She'll have her home duties to attend to."

Bulpert stared at the two separately. Then he rose, pulled at his waistcoat, and went without speaking a word.

"He's took the precaution," remarked Sarah, coming in to clear, as a bang sounded below, "to shut the door after him."

Mrs. Mills, reviewing the party, and expressing the hope that all had enjoyed themselves, mentioned that Miss Rabbit in the course of the evening made a statement to her which had, apparently, been weighing on the lady's mind. Miss Rabbit reproached herself for giving wrong information in regard to the stability of the firm of Hilbert, and begged Mrs. Mills would explain. In her own phrase she tried to out Gertie, and as this had not come off, her suggestion was that bygones should be considered as bygones, and nothing more said about the matter.

"It isn't such a bad world," decided Mrs. Mills, "if you only come to look at it in a good light."

CHAPTER X

Gertie's sympathy with the invalid of Morden Place found itself slightly diminished on Monday morning. The front room had not yet been restored to its normal state, and Mrs. Mills, before rising to start the boy with his delivery of morning newspapers, had given a brief lecture on the drawback of excessive ambition, the advisability of not going on to Land's End when you but held a ticket for Westbourne Park. Ten minutes later she brought upstairs an important-looking envelope that bore her name and address in handwriting which left just the space for the stamp, and Mrs. Mills speculated on the probable contents of the communication until Gertie made the useful suggestion that the envelope should be opened. Mrs. Mills, after reading the letter, flung herself upon the bed and, her head resting on the pillow, sobbed hysterically.

Lady Douglass wrote near the telegram instructions "Private," and, to ensure perfect secrecy, underlined the word three times. Nevertheless, Gertie read it without hesitation, and her first impression was one of regard for the writer's ingenuity. Lady Douglass feared some rumours might have reached Praed Street concerning the behaviour of Miss Higham during the brief stay at Ewelme; unable to rid her mind of this, she was sending a note to assure Mrs. Mills that no grounds whatever existed for the statements. She, herself, had taken great trouble to keep the incident quiet, and could not understand how it had become public property. She hoped Mrs. Mills would believe that Miss Higham had been guilty of nothing more than a want of discretion, natural enough in a girl of her age, and, if Lady Douglass might be allowed to say so, her position in life. Lady Douglass felt it only right to send this note, and hoped her motives would be understood.

"Her motives are clear enough," agreed Gertie. "What I can't quite make out is why she should take so much trouble in going for me. I'm out of her way, and I shan't get into her way again. What more does she want?"

"I'd no idea," wailed her aunt, "that there'd been anything amiss. Of course, I knew you came back Sunday night instead of Monday morning, but you hinted that was because of Clarence. What are the facts, dear?"

Particulars given, Mrs. Mills changed her attitude, both of body and of mind, and announced an intention of starting at once to have it out with her ladyship. A good straight talking to, that was what my lady required, with plain language which included selection of home truths, and Mrs. Mills flattered herself she was the very woman to undertake the task. To this Gertie offered several determined objections. First, Henry's sister-in-law was ill; second, she had endured trouble, and was not perhaps quite herself; third, the incident was ended, and there would be nothing useful in raking up the past. Mrs. Mills listened to the arguments, and agreed to substitute a new resolution—namely, that a reply was to be written couched in terms which could not be charged with the defect of ambiguity.

"I shan't help you with the spelling," declared the girl.

"Somehow or other," complained Mrs. Mills, "you always seem to manage to get everything your own way."

"Not always."

One gratifying result of the evening party came in the fact that Bulpert decreased his visits. For two or three weeks he absented himself from Praed Street; and Mrs. Mills approved this, mentioning as one of the reasons, that it was not wise for an engaged couple to have too much of each other's company. When he did call, Mrs. Mills reported of him that he appeared to have something on his mind; he left before Gertie arrived, and without disclosing the nature of the burden.

As a rule, it happened at Great Titchfield Street that one good contract was followed by a slack period, when the difficulty was to find sufficient work to keep all hands going. But here and now, a high authority ordered some alteration in the uniform of certain of His Majesty's officers of the army, and either Madame or Miss Higham was called frequently to Pall Mall; and, in a brief period, all the outworkers were again busy: Great Titchfield Street found itself so fully occupied that the girls had no time to recall songs learned at the second house of their favourite music hall. Into the hum and activity of this busy hive came, one evening, Madame's husband, making his way to the office where Madame and Miss Higham faced each other at sloping desks. He began to shout; it was clear that on the way from King's Road he had been taking refreshment to encourage determination. When he raised his fist, Gertie stepped forward.

"Miss Higham," said Madame calmly, "I wish you would just run downstairs and fetch a policeman."

Madame's husband instantly showed a diminution of aggressiveness. All he wanted was fair play and reasonable treatment. If there did not happen to be a five-pound note handy, gold would do; failing gold, he must, of course, be content with silver.

"You will go out of this place at once," ordered Madame, in an even voice; "and as a punishment for disobeying my orders, I shall not give you a single penny all this week. I know very well what you want money for. I know what you do with money when I give it to you."

"Impossible to discuss these matt'rs with you," he said, with an effort at haughtiness. "Purely private 'fairs."

"If it wasn't for the business here," she went on, "I think you'd succeed in driving me mad. This just saves me. I'm not going to allow you to interfere with it, and if you dare to come here again, I shall most certainly lock you up. Now be off with you."

Mr. Digby Jacks wept, and, at the doorway, threatened to drown himself in the Thames. In the Thames, just to the right of Cleopatra's Needle.

"I wish you would."

"Shan't, now," he retorted sulkily, "just in order to dis'point you. You're cruel woman, and some day you'll realize it and be sorry. Goo' night, and be hanged to you."

Gertie congratulated Madame upon her firmness, and the other admitted the situation was one not easy to handle. For if, she explained, money had been given, then he would have absented himself from Jubilee Place for a week; as it was, he would be absent for a space of two or three days. Gertie expressed surprise at this behaviour, and Madame said it was almost bound to happen where the wife earned an income, and the husband gained none. By rights, it should be the other way about, and then there was a fair prospect of happiness. Madame counselled the girl to be careful not to imitate the example; Gertie replied that she had long since made up her mind on this point.

"But why don't you get rid of him?" she inquired.

"Because I've left it too long. Besides, I'm too old to get anybody else."

"Surely you'd be better off alone?"

"No, I shouldn't," answered Madame promptly. "What do you make the proper total, my dear, of that account Miss Rabbit made a muddle of?"

Within her experience it had sometimes happened that Gertie, on the way home, found herself spoken to by a stranger; this rarely occurred, because she walked with briskness, and refrained from glancing at other pedestrians. (Generally the intruder was a youth anxious to make or sustain a reputation for gallantry, and he accepted the sharp rebuff with docility.) But news came from Miss Loriner that Lady Douglass, after years of the luxury of imagining herself in delicate health, was now genuinely ill, and Henry went down from town each evening by a late train to make inquiries, returning in the morning. Miss Loriner added that some of Lady Douglass's indisposition might be due to the fact that the executors were hinting at the eventual necessity of taking out probate in regard to Sir Mark's will; this done, a considerable change in affairs was inevitable. In consequence of the information, Gertie could not avoid looking about her in the vague hope of encountering Henry; she wanted to see him, although she knew a meeting would only disturb and confuse. She waited outside the street door after business was over, gazing up and down before making a start for home, and it occurred frequently that a short man of middle age moved a few steps towards her, and stopped; later, in turning out of Portland Place, she observed he was following. Once he came so close that she expected to hear a whining voice complain of space of time since the last meal, and having the superstition that casual charity appeased the gods, she found some coppers; but he fell back, and did not speak. It was at the close of a trying day when the representative of a firm had called, in Madame's absence, to have what he described in a preface as a jolly, thundering good row, which finished by an endeavour on his part to indicate apology by stroking Miss Higham's hand—on this night, Gertie, less composed than usual, again caught sight, in crossing Great Portland Street, of the short man. He turned. She, also turning, met him in the centre of the roadway.

"Do you want to speak to me?" she demanded sharply.

"Not specially," he answered, in a husky voice.

"Then why do you so often follow me about?"

"I hope I don't cause you any ill convenience; if so be as I do, I'll stop it at once."

"That's all right," said Gertie, impressed by his deferential manner. "Only it seemed to me rather odd. And just now my nerves are somewhat jerky." He touched his cap, and was shuffling off, when she recalled him. "Stroll along with me, and let's have a talk. What do you do for a living?"

"Sure you don't mind being seen with me?" he asked.

"We'll go up Great Portland Street, and you can say 'good-bye' when we reach the underground station."

He buttoned his well-worn frock coat, gave himself a brisk punch on the chest, and with every indication of pride, accompanied her, keeping, however, slightly to the rear. Gertie repeated her question, and he replied it was not easy to explain how he gained a livelihood; odd jobs, was perhaps the best answer he could give. Warning her not to be frightened, he gave the information that he had spent fifteen years of his life in prison. Did he begin young, then? No, that was the curious part about it. He had little thought of starting the game until, in one week, he lost his wife and, through the failure of a firm, his employment. Then it seemed to him nothing mattered, and another out-of-work made a suggestion, and he fell into it, was caught, and his friend managed to get away.

"When I came out," he went on, "I found I'd lost all respect for myself, and I assumed everybody else had lost all respect for me. I tell you, it isn't a hard task to go down in this world. I've no business to complain, but there it is; plenty can help you in that direction, but there's very few capable of assisting you to pick yourself up."

"It's not too late to make a change."

"I've got no luck, you see," he explained patiently. "This summer I did nearly get back to what you may call the old style. I was in a reg'lar job; I contrived to dress myself up almost like a duke, and I sets out on Sunday afternoon with the full intention of calling on some old friends I hadn't seen for a good many years. It didn't come off."

"Drink, I suppose."

"Yes," he said. "A chap driving one of these motors had taken a drop too much. I was in St. Mary's in Praed Street for over six weeks. If it had been anybody but me, the car would have been driven by some well-to-do gentleman, and I should have found myself compensated for life. As I say, I never did have my share of good fortune, and I s'pose I never shall. All I haven't had of that, I hope will be passed on to my daughter."

"She ought to do something for you."

"I don't want her to. I've no wish to interfere with her. I can't flatter myself I've done her any good, and I'd like to have the satisfaction of feeling I've done her no harm. Here, I think," looking around him, "we say oh revor."

Gertie took out her purse; he gave an emphatic shake of the head, and went.

The next night he was at the same place, improved in appearance, and Gertie allowed him to accompany her along Marylebone Road so far as Harley Street. On the following evening he furnished an escort to Upper Baker Street, and afterwards extended the journey. His manner was always respectful, and he still made no attempt to walk abreast with her. Sometimes a constable would say, "Hullo, Joe!" and he replied, "Good evening, sir. Not bad weather for the time of year!" and going on, informed Gertie where, and in what circumstances, the acquaintance had been made.

It happened, on one occasion, that Gertie saw Mr. Trew on the box seat of his small brown omnibus coming along from the Great Central Station; he was preparing to flourish a cheery salute, when he caught sight of her companion. Almost dropping his whip, he gave his head a jerk to send the shining silk hat well back, and thus give relief to a suddenly heated brain.

Mrs. Mills was waiting on the Friday evening, some doors east of her own shop; Gertie's new friend did not wait for instructions from his companion, but left her instantly.

"Who's looking after the counter, aunt?"

"Mr. Bulpert," replied the other, panting. "I've give him a cigar to stick in his face. He wants to see you. And I want to see you, too. Who is that you were talking to?"

"The elderly man I told you about. The one who always waits now to see me part of the distance home. Quite a character in his way."

"Quite a bad character," snapped Mrs. Mills.

"Do you know him?"

Her aunt gave a gulp. "I had the word from Mr. Trew," she said, still rather breathless, "and his idea is that you may as well know it now as later on. That man is your father, my dear—your father; and the less you see of him the better. Now, perhaps, you can realize why I knew it was no use letting you carry on with Mr. Douglass. It was bound to come out some day!"

"My father," said the girl slowly and thoughtfully.

"Your very own, dearie. Don't let it upset you more than you can help. I know you've a good deal to put up with just now. Come along and see Mr. Bulpert. A little sweethearting talk will cheer you up."

Bulpert admitted he had one or two questions to put; but on Gertie ordering that they should be offered there and then, he said, gloomily, that some other time would do as well. The girl told him the news just communicated by her aunt, and waited hopefully for the comment; Bulpert remarked, with an indulgent air, that it took all sorts to make a world, and he thought no worse of Gertie because of the fact that she possessed a parent with a spotted record. He offered to see her father and give him a definitely worded warning; the girl answered that the matter could be left in her hands.

"But we don't want him to be a drain on us," he contended. "I know what these individuals are like. Species of blackmail, that's what it amounts to. And I don't wish to see you working your fingers to the bone, and a certain proportion of the money earned being paid out to him. I couldn't bear it, so I tell you straight!" He slapped a pile of magazines on the counter.

"I'm rather worried," she said, "and I don't want any more misunderstandings. I told you not long ago I shouldn't go back to Great Titchfield Street once I was married."

"That's what I wanted to speak to you about. You're not serious, I s'pose, in saying this. You're only doing it to test my affection."

"I mean every word."

"Very well!" announced Bulpert defiantly. "Understand, then, that the engagement's off. Entirely and absolutely off. And if you're so ill-advised as to bring an action for breach, you jolly well can. Won't be a bad advert, for a public man like F. W. B. It'll get him talked about!"

CHAPTER XI

The final departure of Bulpert erased a troublesome detail in the girl's life, and she felt suitably thankful; another disappearance gave her a sensation of regret. She had thought seriously of the patient, elderly man whom she had now to look upon as her parent, and planned a scheme, to be prefaced by something in the nature of a brief lecture, involving pecuniary sacrifice; her game of bricks was knocked over by the hand of Fate, and Gertie Higham had to put them back into the box. Mrs. Mills told her much that had hitherto been a secret shared by Mr. Trew.

"Quite a good sort he was, my dear, until your poor young mother went, and then—well, Mr. Trew met him when he came out of Wormwood Scrubbs, and your father's first words were, 'Don't let the kid ever know!' Meaning yourself. So we kept it from you, you see, and I hope you don't blame us. No doubt, he recognized you, because you're so much like your poor mother, only more stylish, and of course better educated, and I suppose he felt as though he had to speak. Very likely he won't ever let you see him again."

"Wish I knew where to find him now."

"He was like a lot of the others. Not really bad, you understand, but just rather easily led; and because he thought everything was going against him, he became reckless. And he belonged to the old days when once in prison meant always in prison, and no one ever thought that a man who had made a single blunder could be reformed. I often used to think," declared Mrs. Mills, "that something ought to be done, but of course I had my business to look after."

"You found time to look after me, aunt."

"If you could realize," argued the other earnestly, "what a dear baby you was then, you wouldn't trouble to give me any credit for that." She hesitated. "What I've always hoped," lowering her voice, "that some day I might see another one like you."

"Madame's case," said Gertie, "is a warning to me. I want the right kind of husband, or none at all!"

From Clarence Mills, calling at Praed Street, came news that Lady Douglass had been instructed to go abroad so soon as she became well enough to endure the journey; to his great concern, Miss Loriner was instructed to accompany her. Gertie asked for further information, and Clarence replied that Henry Douglass had not given up the office in Old Quebec Street; indeed, he recently entered a competition for plans of a provincial art gallery, and his portrait was in some journal consequent on the decision of the judges. Gertie presumed that Clarence did not happen to have this with him; Clarence found the cutting in his letter-case and presented it. (Later, it was mounted carefully and placed in a small frame, and given a position upon her dressing-table.) Clarence's book was out, and he had just seen a copy at Paddington, with a card bearing the words, "Tremendously Thrilling."

On another point, Clarence was able to announce that Henry had held something like a court-martial at Ewelme, with all concerned present. Jim Langham gave evidence; and Lady Douglass, when her turn came, suggested the key had been placed in her bag by Miss Loriner. Upon which Miss Loriner declared it would be impossible, in view of this remark, to give her company to Beaulieu; and Lady Douglass, without any further hesitation, confessed the truth, urging, in excuse, that it was but natural in this world to look after oneself, adding a caution to the effect that anything in the nature of a scene would now mar the work of the London specialist. Henry's mother, it appeared, was in favour of taking the risk.

"I don't want to see her punished," remarked Gertie. "So long as he knows I was not to blame, I'm perfectly satisfied."

Clarence had private audience with Mrs. Mills before going, and, as a result, Sarah, the temporary assistant at the party, came to Praed Street daily; Mrs. Mills admitted that, seeing her niece frequently, any want of colour might not be so apparent to her as to any one who saw the girl less often. Sarah's objections to living in were easy to meet; the only other provision was that liberty should be given if her services were required for "Puss in Boots" during the Christmas period. An excellent worker, Sarah left nothing to be done at the end of the day, and Gertie, arriving home after the stress of business at Great Titchfield Street, was able to rest in the parlour, or give assistance in the shop.

She was making out orders for Christmas cards at the newspaper counter one night (the popular remark of customers at this period was "Ain't the evenings drawing in something awful!") when a man rushed in and looked around in a dazed, frightened manner. He muttered indistinctly some explanation, and was going off, when Gertie called to him.

"Thought it was a bar," he said confusedly. "My mistake."

"Come here, Mr. Langham," she ordered, putting down her book. "Sit on the high chair." He obeyed, blinking up at the light. "What's the matter?"

Jim Langham was trembling. He leaned across, and whispered.

"You've seen a ghost?" she echoed. "Don't be so stupid. There are no such things nowadays, especially in a neighbourhood like this. Where did you come across it?"

"Near—near the station. I've only just come from Wallingford. I was hurrying up the slope on the right-hand side, and about to turn into the hotel, when across the way—"

He looked around apprehensively, and caught sight of Mrs. Mills peeping over the half blind of the parlour door. Gertie sent her a reassuring nod, and she disappeared.

"What have I done," he wailed appealingly, "that everybody should spy? A police sergeant gazed at me in a most peculiar way about two minutes ago. What does it mean, Miss Higham?"

"Doesn't matter what it means," she said sharply, "so long as you've done nothing wrong. Pull yourself together, Mr. Langham. Why don't you knock off the drink, and be a man?"

"I'll go and get some now."

"It will do you no good. You've been in the habit of taking it when you didn't need it, and you've spoilt it as a remedy. Stay here for a while, and calm yourself."

"Bad enough," he complained, "when living people begin to track you about, but when the others start doing it—!" He shivered. Gertie went to the parlour, and asked her aunt to make some coffee.

"Has Lady Douglass gone away yet?"

"Now why, apropos of nothing, should you mention her name?"

"You never did have much sense about you, and now you seem to have none at all. Concentrate your mind. Think! What was the question I put to you?" He admitted he could not recall it, and she repeated the inquiry.

"Leaves early to-morrow morning," he answered; "that is partly why I have come up to town. I don't want to see her again before she goes." Jim Langham rested elbows on the counter, and covered eyes with his hands. "Have you ever," he asked, "in the course of your existence, met with a bigger fool than me?"

"To be quite candid," said Gertie, "I don't think I have."

She fetched the cup from the back room, and brought it to him. He sipped at the hot beverage, and appeared to recover.

"Do you mind if I smoke?" he asked courteously.

She laughed. "This is half a tobacconist's shop!"

"Quite so," remarked Jim Langham, taking a cigar from his case. "I say," he went on confidentially, taking the movable gas jet, "do you know anything about the Argentine?"

"Mr. Trew might tell you something about it if he were here. I don't take any interest in horse-racing."

"It's a place in South America," he said. "I've an idea of getting out there, and making a fresh start. But I'm in the state of mind that prevents me from knowing how to set about it. It would be a great kindness on your part to give me some assistance."

"I want all the money I've saved up."

He placed his hand in his waistcoat pocket and pulled out sovereigns. Gertie, taking a newspaper, turned the pages to find the shipping advertisements.

"'The R. M. S. P.,'" she read. "I thought that meant you had to reply to an invitation. Oh, I see. Royal Mail Steam Packet. Here's the address. There's a boat leaving to-morrow. Would you like to catch that?"

"The earlier the better," he cried. "I must get away at once. Now, who can do it all?"

A lad came for a packet of cigarettes, and, as Gertie served him, Mr. Trew entered the doorway; his cheerful salutation caused Jim Langham to start. Trew announced, joyously, that he was up to the neck in trouble; for failing to see a young constable's warning in Oxford Street, he had been suspended from duty for a period of three days.

"As I told him, if a driver took notice of all the baby hands held up, why the 'bus would never reach Victoria. Howsomever, here I am; my own master for a time, and ready to make myself generally useless. What about a half-day excursion to Brighton to-morrow, little missy?"

"This, Mr. Trew, is Mr. Langham."

"I don't get on over and above first class," he said, "with a certain relative of yours, sir, but I never met a family yet that was all alike. Some white sheep in every flock."

Gertie explained Jim Langham's requirements, and Trew, placing his hat upon the counter, and admitting himself to be something of an authority on matters connected with the sea, brought his best intelligence to bear upon the subject. It was too late, he decided, to go down that evening to the steamship office, but a telegram might be sent, asking for a berth to be reserved, and Mr. Langham could go to the docks in the morning.

"It is absolutely imperative," declared the other urgently, "that I leave at the first possible moment."

"If the worst comes to the worst," said Mr. Trew, "you can ship as a stowaway. You come up on deck, third day out, and kneel at the captain's feet and sing a song about being an orphan. That, of course, would be a last resource."

Gertie discovered a telegram form, and on the instructions of Mr. Trew, filled it in; and Jim Langham assured her that he was more obliged than he could express in words. Mr. Trew left to arrange the dispatch of the message.

"I count myself extremely fortunate," said the other, "to have encountered you, Miss Higham. If you hear anything against me later on, I—I should feel grateful if you thought the best of me that you can. I wish," he went on, with an anxious air, "I wish I knew how to repay you."

"Don't make a fuss about trifles," she recommended.

He gazed at a picture of a well-attired youth smoking a cigar.

"I was a decent chap once," he said thoughtfully, "but that was long ago. Look here, Miss Higham! Henry—you know Henry?"

"I did know him." Turning her face away.

"He will be at Paddington Station tomorrow morning at ten. See him there. Put off every other engagement, and see him."

"There will be no use in doing that."

"There may be," he contradicted earnestly. "You've been very hard hit over this business, and I happen to know he wants to meet you, only that he is afraid of appearing intrusive. At ten o'clock at the arrival platform. May I say good-bye now? God bless you. I haven't much influence with Him, but I—I hope He'll be good to you!"

She came from behind the counter, and accompanied him to the swing doors.

"Whose ghost was it you thought you saw, Mr. Langham?"

"I must have been mistaken," he replied vaguely. "A shame to have worried you!"

All the comedy in life and some of the tragedy can be found at London railway stations, and only the fact that members of the staff are well occupied prevents them from furnishing shelves of bookstalls with records of their observation. The classes are there (an effort is being made to cancel one useful intermediate stage), presenting themselves, for the most part, in a highly-agitated condition of mind, with the result that officials acquire the methods of those who deal with the mentally unhinged; show themselves prepared for any display of eccentricity. Ever, as in life, you remark the people who arrive too soon, or too late; a few lucky ones come in the very nick of time. The last named are favourites, selected with no obvious reason by Fortune, and greatly envied by their contemporaries; it is usual for them to claim the entire credit to themselves. Apart from these, at the terminal stations where no barriers exist, are folk who make but little affectation of being passengers, and use the station as a playground, with engine and train for toys.

To Paddington at a quarter to ten in the morning came hurriedly, although there was no cause for hurry, Gertie Higham, escorted by Mr. Trew, both exceptionally costumed as befitting a notable occasion. Gertie's escort had a pair of driving-gloves, and he could not determine whether it looked more aristocratic to wear these or to carry them with a negligent air; he compromised on the departure platform by wearing one and carrying the other. The collector-dog trotted up with the box on his back, and both put in some coppers. They glanced at the giant clock.

"I wish," she said agitatedly, "that I could skip half an hour of my life."

"When you get to my age, little missy," remarked Trew, "you won't talk like that. Speaking personally, I can fairly say that if it wasn't for these new motors I sh'd like to live to be a 'underd. Now, let's jest make sure and certain about this train."

"I thought we had done so."

"May as well be on the safe side."

Mr. Trew left her at the bookstall to go on a journey in search of verification. She observed that he obtained news first from a junior porter, and worked upwards in the scale, with the evident intention of obtaining at last corroborative evidence from a director. The girl turned, and, gazing at the rows of books, found she could not read the titles clearly. One of the lads of the stall came with a book in his hand, recommending it to her notice; written by a new chap, he mentioned confidentially, and highly interesting. Gertie pulled herself together, and gave attention.

"Thank you," she said, "but it's the work of a cousin of mine."

The lad put Clarence Mills's novel down, and took up a pocket edition of "Merchant of Venice."

"In that case," he remarked, "I suppose it's no use showing you anything written by your Uncle William."

Trew came at a run, saving her the necessity of thinking of an answer. Mr. Henry was now on the arrival platform, right across where a finger pointed; Gertie was to wait until a scarlet handkerchief showed itself, and she begged him very earnestly not to give the signal unless it appeared to be well justified. A train, that had received no education in the art of reticence, came to an intervening set of lines, and Gertie's anxiety increased; she hurried down the platform to a point from which it was possible to see the meeting. Henry was engaged in conversation with a Great Western official; Mr. Trew, in going past, turned and, with a great air of wonder, recognized him. Gertie noted with satisfaction that Henry's greeting was hearty and unrestrained. Mr. Trew indicated a superior carriage standing near; she knew, from his gestures, that he was describing the uncovered conveyances recalled from his early youth.

"Oh, do make haste!" she urged under her breath.

They moved a few steps together, and Henry interrupted conversation with an inquiry. Mr. Trew, astonished to the extent of taking off his hat, gave a wave with it in the direction of Platform Number One, and Henry spoke eagerly. Mr. Trew took out his scarlet handkerchief, rubbed his face.

"Now," cried Henry, advancing delightedly to meet her, "I wonder what the chances were against our meeting here?"

"It is rather unexpected, isn't it?"

"Where," he hesitated, "where is Mr. Bulpert?"

"I really don't know," she replied, smiling. "We're not engaged any longer."

"Good news!" he cried with emphasis. "That is to say, it's good news if you wished the engagement to cease."

"I wasn't sorry."

He took her elbow, and glanced around. Mr. Trew was examining a set of milk churns with the air of an experienced dairyman.

"Isn't it amazing," said Henry, "how one lucky moment can change the appearance of everything? I've been feeling lately that nothing could possibly come right, and now—"

"We mustn't go on too fast," she interposed sagely, "because that only means more disappointment. You haven't heard yet about my father. Listen whilst I tell you about him."

Gertie waited, as she went on, for a relaxation in the pleasant hold on her arm, but this did not come. When she had said the last word, he nodded.

"I knew all about this long before you did," he said. "The information came from my sister-in-law. She had discovered the facts, and felt disappointed, I think, to find that I was not greatly impressed. Of course, you're not responsible for his actions any more than I can be held liable for the behaviour of Jim Langham. Jim is a much worse nut than your father; he hasn't any excuse for his conduct. Forged his sister's name to a big cheque, and, naturally, he has disappeared. I am giving him time to get away before I say anything about it to her."

"May be leaving England now, I suppose?"

"I hope so; but we needn't bother about him. Let us talk about ourselves, just as we used to do. Do you remember, dear girl?"

"I recollect it," she admitted. "Every moment, and every step, and every word. It will always be something good for me to look back upon, when I'm older."

He bent down to her. "We'll look back upon it together," he said affectionately.

"No!"

The official to whom Henry had been speaking begged pardon for interrupting; the train, he announced, would be about five minutes late. Gertie thanked him with a glance that, at any honestly managed exchange office, could be converted into bank notes.

"Has your view of me altered, then?" he asked.

"My view of you," she replied steadily, "is exactly the same that it always has been, ever since I first met you. I like you better—oh, a lot better—than any one else in the world, and I know that if you married me you'd do all you could to make me happy and comfortable. But I shouldn't be happy and comfortable. I've got to look forward; and when I do that, there's no use in shutting my eyes. I can see quite clearly what would happen. You'd have this large house down in the country, and you would ask friends there, and I should make blunders, and, sooner or later, you'd be certain to feel ashamed of me."

"I don't agree, dear," he said with emphasis. "Anyhow let us try the experiment. I am sure you overestimate the distance between us. Think how well we used to get along together."

"If life was all summer evenings and Primrose Hill," she remarked, "I might stand a chance. But it isn't. Your life is going to be that of a country gentleman in Berkshire; my life is going to be that of a well-paid worker in Great Titchfield Street."

"Wish I could find some method," he cried vehemently, "of giving events a twist. I'd much rather go on in my own profession. I'm making my way slowly, but I'm making it for myself, and I—I want you for company." He gave a gesture of appeal. "Can't you see how much it means?"

"We've got to take matters as they are, and not as we should like them to be. And it isn't as though I'd only got myself to think about. There's you. If I didn't care so much for you, it might be different."

"For the moment," protested Henry Douglass, "I find myself wishing, dear, that you were not quite so sensible. We will talk about this again, won't we? Let me call at Praed Street."

"Rather you didn't," said Gertie, "if you don't mind, because I shall never change my decision. And I wish I could explain how sorry I am it hasn't all come right." She looked up at him with tears in her eyes. "Give me a kiss before we say good-bye."

"We're to say a lot of other things to each other," he asserted determinedly, "but we are never to say that! Stay here, until I have seen these people into the railway omnibus. Please!"

The train came slowly; the engine with the air of one that had, in its time, hurt itself by violent contact with buffers; a line of porters edged the platform, ready to seize brass handles of compartments so soon as the train stopped. Gertie stood behind a trolley, and watched the crowd of alighting passengers. She caught sight of Lady Douglass and Miss Loriner: Lady Douglass carrying her small dog, and apparently more authoritative than ever in manner; her companion nursing a copy of Clarence's book. Henry and Rutley went to the rear van to see to the luggage, and presently returned; Rutley talked animatedly, Henry's features exhibited surprise. The railway omnibus was found; transfer of luggage began.

"My dearest, dearest!" cried Henry excitedly. "Listen to me; hear the great news Rutley has brought. My brother arrived home last night. The good fellow is safe and sound. He came down from here, from Paddington, and called at Ewelme to get some important papers he wanted. Heard Lady Douglass's voice—she happened to be annoyed about something—and left without seeing her. This means—don't you see?—that I have nothing now to bother about, excepting my work. And you!"

She had a difficulty in finding words. "Mr. Langham did not meet a ghost, then."

"I'm going to see the boat train off at Victoria," he went on rapidly, "and I shall be back at Praed Street in an hour. Less than an hour. We'll go out to lunch together."

"I'll wait for you there!" promised the happy girl.

William Pett Ridge – A Short Biography

William Pett Ridge was born at Chartham, near Canterbury, Kent, on 22nd April 1859.

His family's resources were certainly limited. His father was a railway porter, and the young Pett Ridge, after schooling in Marden, Kent became a clerk in a railway clearing-house. The hours were long and arduous, but self-improvement was Pett Ridge's goal. After working from nine until seven o'clock he would attend evening classes at Birkbeck Literary and Scientific Institute and then to follow his passion; the ambition to write. He was heavily influenced by Dickens and several critics thought he had the capability to be his successor.

From 1891 many of his humourous sketches were published in the St James's Gazette, the Idler, Windsor Magazine and other literary periodicals of the day.

Pett Ridge published his first novel in 1895, A Clever Wife. By the advent of his fifth novel, Mord Em'ly, a mere three years later in 1898, his success was obvious. His writing was written from the perspective of those born with no privilege and relied on his great talent to find humour and sympathy in his portrayal of working class life.

Today Pett Ridge and other East End novelists including Arthur Nevinson, Arthur Morrison and Edwin Pugh are being grouped together as the Cockney Novelists.

In 1924, Pugh set out his recollections of Pett Ridge from the 1890s: "I see him most clearly, as he was in those days, through a blue haze of tobacco smoke. We used sometimes to travel together from Waterloo to Worcester Park on our way to spend a Saturday afternoon and evening with H. G. Wells. Pett Ridge does not know it, but it was through watching him fill his pipe, as he sat opposite me in a stuffy little railway compartment, that I completed my own education as a smoker... Pett Ridge had a small, dark, rather spiky moustache in those days, and thick, dark, sleek hair which is perhaps not quite so thick or dark, though hardly less sleek nowadays than it was then".

With his success, on the back of his prolific output and commercial success, Pett Ridge gave generously of both time and money to charity. In 1907 he founded the Babies Home at Hoxton. This was one of several organisations that he supported that had the welfare of children as their mission.

His circle considered Pett Ridge to be one of life's natural bachelors. In 1909 They were rather surprised therefore when he married Olga Hentschel.

As the 1920's arrived Pett Ridge added to his popularity with the movies. Four of his books were adapted into films.

Pett Ridge now found the peak of his fame had passed. Although he still managed to produce a book a year he was falling out of fashion and favour with the reading public and his popularity declined rapidly. His canon runs to over sixty novels and short-story collections as well as many pieces for magazines and periodicals.

William Pett Ridge died, on 29th September 1930, at his home, Ampthill, Willow Grove, Chislehurst, at the age of 71.

He was cremated at West Norwood on 2nd October 1930.

Minor Dialogues (1895)
A Clever Wife (1895)
An Important Man and Others (1896)
Second Opportunity of Mr Staplehurst (1896)
Mord Em'ly (1898)
Outside The Radius. Stories of a London suburb (1899)
A Son of the State (1899)
A Breaker of Laws (1900)
London Only. A Set Of Common Occurrences (1901)
Lost Property (1902)
Up Side Streets – Short Stories (1903)
Erb (1903)
George And The General (1904)
Next Door Neighbours (1904)
Mrs Galer's Business (1905)
The Wickhamses (1906)
Name of Garland (1907)
Speaking Rather Seriously (1908)
Sixty Nine Birnam Road (1908)
Table d'Hôte. Tales (1910)
Splendid Brother (1910)
From Nine to Six-Thirty (1910)
Light Refreshment (1911)
Thanks to Sanderson (1911)
Love at Paddington (1912)
Devoted Sparkes (1912)
The Remington Sentence (1913)
Mixed Grill (1913)
The Happy Recruit (1914)
The Kennedy People (1915)
Book Here – Short Stories (1915)
Stray Thoughts from W. Pett Ridge (1916)
Madam Prince (1916)
The Amazing Years (1917)
Special Performance (1918)
Well To Do Arthur (1920)
Just Open. Short Stories (1920)
Richard Triumphant (1922)
Lunch Basket – Tales (1923)
Miss Mannering (1923)
Rare Luck (1924)
Leaps And Bounds (1924)
A Story Teller – Forty Years In London (1923)

Just Like Aunt Bertha (1925)
I Like To Remember (1925)
Our Mr Willis (1926)
London Types Taken From Life (1926)
Easy Distances (1927)
The Two Mackenzies (1928)
The Slippery Ladder (1929)
Eldest Miss Collingwood (1930)
Led by Westmacott (1931)

William Pett Ridge also wrote a play titled "Four small plays"

www.ingramcontent.com/pod-product-compliance
Lightning Source LLC
Chambersburg PA
CBHW021937170626
46807CB00007B/3154